THE SONS OF CROSBY BOOK 1

KATHI S. BARTON

This is a work of fiction. Names, characters, places, and incidents are products of the author's imagination or are used fictitiously and are not to be construed as real. Any resemblance to actual events, locations, organizations, or persons, living or dead, is entirely coincidental.

World Castle Publishing, LLC
Pensacola, Florida
Copyright © Kathi S. Barton 2017
Paperback ISBN: 9781629897165
eBook ISBN: 9781629897172
First Edition World Castle Publishing, LLC, June 12, 2017
http://www.worldcastlepublishing.com
Licensing Notes
All rights reserved. No part of this book may be used or reproduced in any manner whatsoever without written permission, except in the case of brief quotations embodied in articles and reviews.
Cover: Karen Fuller
Editor: Maxine Bringenberg

PROLOGUE

The woman in his arms was weak. Crosby wasn't sure that she was going to make it, not the way she'd been burned. As soon as he laid her on the soft earth, she opened her eyes and looked up at him. Crosby felt his heart skip several beats. My goodness, she sure was a pretty little thing.

"The others?" He told her that his sons were getting out as many as they could. "Thank you. The house, it just exploded into flames. We had no time to get out."

"We caught him." She frowned, but let her eyes flutter closed. Asking her if she was all right enough for him to leave her for a moment, she nodded. Crosby went to the house to help his boys.

They had no way of knowing how many faeries were inside the house. A few of them had died, either from smoke inhalation or fire. They pulled out as many as they could, dead or alive, and laid them on the ground. Soon there'd be nothing left of the building, but he didn't want to leave anyone behind if he could help it. The faeries, even the smaller ones, were worth any kind of pain they might get from the hot flames to save them.

"They're all out, so far as we can tell. We've made an area

over there for the dead. The ones that can be saved are being helped by the others." Jason, his oldest, dropped to his knees. "I don't think we missed anyone, but it's burning too hot for us to go back in. I'm sorry, Dad."

"We did the best we could, son. You have to believe that. That house, it went up fast. I'm thinking that the man who did this, he knew what he was about." He glanced over at the woman he'd brought out. She was resting, which he was glad for. And her body seemed to be healing slowly. "I think she'd be the one in charge. If she's awake, ask her how many were in the place, please."

Jason stood just as the rest of them were coming out of the falling down building. Just as the last of his boys walked out, the entire thing collapsed. Grayson jumped back when his shirt caught on one of the embers. Luckily, Elliot was able to help him out.

Crosby dropped to the ground and counted his blessings after verifying all his sons were safe. He didn't want them hurt either. This had been a hell of a night so far.

They'd simply been walking along the path, none of them in any kind of hurry, when they'd heard the blast, followed by screams. Even as far away as they'd been, nearly two miles, he'd heard them in pain. The man, running from the scene and smelling like death, was caught and taken back. His confession was also his death warrant. Jason had snapped his neck and left him where he lay.

Jason returned with the woman walking slowly next to him. She looked a good deal better than she had when he'd found her, and she was wearing Jason's shirt. Sitting down between the two of them, she thanked him again for his service. He told her it was his pleasure and waved away her offer of a reward.

"It wasn't anything for us to come to your aid, my lady. We were just out and about when we smelled the smoke. The house, well, it was over almost as soon as we got here." She nodded. "I'm sorry about your family, miss. There was no cause for this."

"You said that he'd been caught. Is he...did you kill him?" Crosby told her that he was dead, yes. "Thank you for that. Had he been able to get away, I fear that he would do more of the same to my kind. I wish to repay you."

"No, that won't be necessary. I know what you are and what they were, but we've no desire to take anything else from you. You have lost enough, my lady." She nodded and Crosby introduced her to his sons. "This is Jason, my oldest. Then in order of birth to youngest, it's Chase, Elliot, Grayson, Ryan, and the youngest is Sean. This is the Lady Kilian, the faerie queen."

He was proud of his sons, though they were men now, they were still his little boys. As they shook her hand he spoke of them, just little things that he was happy to share with her. How they'd been taking lessons from the neighbor lady to learn how to sew and knit. Things that men should know how to do in the event of an emergency. How Sean could do some doctoring if necessary, even on a human. All notes of the pride that Crosby felt for his sons. When she turned to him, he could see that she had completely healed and was feeling like herself again. She looked at the dead and injured.

"The man who did this, he was out to kill all of us." Crosby said that was about right. "Had you not come here when you did, he would have succeeded. By killing me, without someone to take my place as the queen, all faeries would have perished. And you know as well as I, that would be the death of a great deal of magic."

"We only came to help out the people living here, miss. We would have done the same for anyone." She smiled at him. "You're very beautiful, my lady. I'm glad that we could save you and the others. I'm sorry that there wasn't more time for us. We'll help with the dead, should you wish. As I said, it won't be any trouble at all."

"You have given the world around us a great gift, Crosby. As well as your sons. Because of your bravery, only a few died rather than all of us." Crosby nodded, but felt embarrassed. "I have given a gift to your sons, and now I shall do the same for you. 'Tis only a touch to give to you, but I should like more."

He didn't know what to expect from her. But when she wrapped her arms around him, Crosby felt his entire body shake with it. She was giving him something, something that he did not deserve but was going to get anyway. And as his sons fell to the ground when he was released, he watched as she staggered to them then dropped herself. Christ, whatever she'd done to them, they'd be lucky to make it home before the sun rose. It would be just about his luck to save faeries from a fire only to be burned up by the sun rising.

"You will be fine, Crosby. All of you will." He was still too sick to wonder what she was talking about as he lay back on the grass. His head was still spinning, and he was slightly sick to his stomach. "I will leave you to rest now so that I might take care of the wounded and our dead."

Crosby looked at his sons, each of them laying there as if they were dead. He knew that they weren't, he could hear each of their hearts beating. As the sun crested over the mountain, he tried to stand. Getting to his boys was much harder than he thought it should be after a simple thank you gift. Every inch he crawled toward them, it felt as if he was taken several feet back. Christ, he was going to die right there.

"Dad?" He nodded at Jason as he got to his knees too. "I'm sick. I mean, I feel like I need to puke and my legs are weak. What did she do to us?"

"She said it was a gift. For saving her and the others. Doesn't feel that way, but that's what she told me." Jason cursed as he stood up on his wobbly legs. "We have to get to shelter. Can you get the others going?"

"I'm not hurt." He looked at Sean, who was standing with his arms wide. He wanted to tell him to grab up one of the others and go, but he looked at him, with the sunlight streaming behind him, and didn't see any blisters. His skin wasn't peeling back. And he looked...Well, he looked happy. "The sun isn't hurting me. I bet it's not going to hurt any of us. And it feels fantastic."

Crosby looked at his own hands. They were covered in soot but not from his own flesh. Wiping them on his pants, he noticed that he wasn't blistered either. His skin was just like it was when he was indoors, hiding from the very thing that would end their lives. Looking at the sun, he felt the warmth of it on his face and none of the terror that usually came with being outside. He'd not felt this good, this warm, for as long as he could remember.

"She gave us the gift of sunlight." Crosby nodded at Jason. "Do you think that it's only for today? I mean, if it is, then I want to stay out here all through it. I have never felt the sun before."

No, neither had he. Once, long ago, he'd felt it for a fleeting moment when his wife had died. It had been in his heart to join her, but the boys had needed him. And the promise that he'd made to her before her passing had made him go into hiding again. He missed Rena every day.

He'd lost his wife to beast. Not a human, but just as bad. There were a few good humans—he wasn't stupid enough to think that they'd all come from the same mold—but when they were bad, they were murderous. The creature had torn her throat out, for no other reason than that he could. Crosby had felt her death like his own heart had stopped beating along with her.

They did stay in the sun all day. He'd been worried for a bit when Elliot had started to burn. But it turned out to be nothing more than too much sun. A strange feeling for a vampire, even as old as he was. Crosby was able to get them to rest a bit, knowing deep in his heart that this was going to make it harder for them to go back to the darkness. But it was so much fun for them. They'd even made their way to the little pond behind their lair.

Swimming with the sun beating down on them burned their tender skin a little more. He'd been sore for about a minute, then it wore off. He was going to tan, he thought, the funniest thing he'd ever thought of. But relaxing in the sun-warmed water was a heavenly feeling, one that he'd never forget.

By nightfall they were all exhausted. There hadn't been any need for them to rest during the day, and he thought they'd have to pay for it later, but he could have no more told them no than he could have told himself. Being in the sunlight, while fleeting, was the most fun he'd had in a very long time.

Crosby loved his children. All six of them. They had kept

him going these last decades without their mother. He was tired, however. Not just today due to how special it had been for them all, but he was tired of living. They no longer needed him, they had proven that to him over and over. Tomorrow night, he decided, he'd talk to them and tell him of his plans. It was well past time for him to join their beloved mother.

CHAPTER 1

Chase let the water fall over his body. It had been a long day, and he was frankly sick of trying to make things right in the business world when others only wanted to make it work for them. He supposed that he wanted the same thing, for it to work the way he wanted, just not only for profits. He wanted to keep businesses working so that people could. Taking the bottle of shampoo from the shelf above his head, he washed all the stink out of his hair first, then off his body.

Getting out after turning off the water, he thought of what he was going to say to Jason. He and his older brother were meeting at his house and then going to get some dinner. Dinner. It still had a strange feeling for him when he thought about actually having a meal.

Chase was pulling on his pants when his dad came into the room.

"You know what I hate more than anything in this world?" Chase told him living. "No. Why would you say that to me?"

"Because it's all you complain about. How the faerie queen took advantage of your good nature and kindness and kept you from Mom. We get it...you don't want to be hanging around us anymore." Chase pulled a dress shirt from his closet and was putting it on when he came out of his closet again. "What's wrong now?"

"You really don't think that, do you?" Chase said nothing. "You really do. You think I don't want to spend time with you boys anymore. I love you, son. All of you."

"Dad, I'm nearly two thousand years old, so I think you can stop calling me a boy. And since we saved the queen over six hundred years ago now, you've done nothing but bitch about how she kept you from meeting the sun when you wanted to join Mom. What else do you suppose we should surmise from that?" His dad sat down but Chase didn't join him. "I'm going to meet Jason for a dinner meeting."

"Chase?" He stopped on the stairs and looked up at his dad. He looked upset; more than that, he looked like he was going to cry. Something he'd never seen him do before, not even when they felt their mom passing. "I'd like to ask you a quick question. Then if you don't mind, I'd like to go to dinner too."

"You can go with us, but I have to leave now. Jason doesn't like to be late for anything, even if it's just food." His dad came down the stairs. "What is it you wanted to ask me?"

"I'll ask you when we meet up with Jason. Are the rest of your brothers going to be there?" He told him he didn't think so, but he'd not made the plans, Jason had. "Well, if you don't mind, I'll have them come along. I miss them."

Chase drove to the offices and let himself in with his dad. There were a few people still wandering around, but they didn't stop to talk to them. He was late enough as it was. As soon as he entered the big conference room, Jason looked at his watch.

"I had to clean that shit off me from today." Jason and Dad took their seats and Chase sat across from them. "The

14

bargaining for the business has gone south. They don't want to change anything. And because of that, they're not going to be able to hit the balloon payment next month when it's due, and reasoning with them is useless. They've been doing it their way for too long, I was told, to change things now."

"Exactly what I told Mr. Canada when he called me today to complain about you. He said that you had a one-track mind and that he didn't care for it. I told him that had he gotten off the track that he was on for one moment, they'd not have to borrow money to pay for payroll or to get caught up on their improvements." Jason slid a file at him. "The balloon payment won't be made, just as you said, and then we'll move in and take the plant. As much as I hate to do that, I don't think there is any other way for it to work."

"Is this the warehouse that is on Main Street?" Jason told Dad that it was, that they manufactured small baking pans and nothing more. "I see. And these baking pans, they're of good quality? They sell well?"

"Oh yes, but not as many as they used to sell, for the simple reason that they're so well made that they can be passed on from generation to generation. That's the reason that we were trying to get them to expand their line to larger pans as well as other shapes. To open a newer market." Chase handed his dad the mockups that they'd made for the plant as Jason continued. "They sold, at one time, nearly six million pans a year all over the world. They've had this market cornered for decades, but now, as I said, they've saturated the customer base and have no one else to sell to."

"And these are what you wanted them to make?" Jason told Dad how that was only the beginning and the easiest to do. There was little need to change out their lines for such a small difference. "The owner, he's the man who makes them? I mean, his family is the one that owns this place?"

"Yes. Not the original family member. His family has been doing this since before this man, Mr. Charles Canada, was born." Dad nodded and picked up the specs on the pan. "What are you thinking, Dad? You have an idea to get him to change his mind?"

"I do, but it will be dishonest." He asked him how. "Well, I know that these can be made for a fraction of the cost in another country. Not as good, nor will they last all that long. You know that as well. What if, and this is the dishonest part, we tell them that in order to recoup our losses on this, we have to sell this idea to someone that will make them? Or that when we take over the plant—which like you say, we'll have to if he won't play ball—that we'll make them and put our own name on them? He won't like that any better than he does change, but at least we can try that."

"You think to trick him into doing this?" Dad told him it was worth a try. "I like it. I mean, it's not so much dishonest as it is just being harsh on what we wanted him to do in the first place. And maybe we will make them show some profit."

"Could be he'll just roll over. So, you might want to play the family aspect of this. Tell him it's a real shame that his name isn't going to be around much when these pans come out. I'm not sure of the wording, but you can figure that out." Dad started to pace the long room and talk at the same time. "You could even tell him that you'll have to fire all the employees. Something about them being set in their ways because he was. That would make me sit up and take notice. Didn't you say something a few weeks back about him having employees that have been there for nearly thirty years?"

"Two that have been there for fifty. Nearly ready to retire, but if we take over, they'll have nothing." Jason was making notes as Chase fed him information that he'd found out this week working at the plant. "You were right about the building too. The improvements to the walls and bathrooms has made a huge difference in the way things flow. Also, the idea that we suggested for putting in a cafeteria was an excellent one. We could bring in some food carts for now, that way we can have them start to like hot food often enough that it will defray the costs of the improvement."

"I like this. I'll work on it tonight and then go and see him in the morning." Jason stood up and so did Chase. Their dad was still sitting after pacing for a few more minutes. "Dad? Are you going? The rest of them are meeting us at the restaurant."

"Yes, of course. I hope that it's all right that I invited them." Jason said it was. "Good. I asked if they could come, and they wanted to know what it was about. I need to talk to you all."

"All right. And all they asked me when they linked with me was where we were going. Ryan is upping the reservation to seven instead of two." Jason looked at Dad and Chase just shrugged. "What's going on?"

"Do you think that I don't want to hang out with you boys anymore?" Chase sat down, thinking this was going to be long and drawn out. They all knew that their dad was unhappy with not being able to meet the sun. "I'm asking because it was brought to my attention that I bitch about not wanting to be alive a great deal."

"You do. And yes, I'm sure that the rest of us feel that way as well. We've talked about it, trying to figure out a way to make you want to be around for us, and we've given up, I think. You just don't want to be happy with being alive." Dad nodded and looked at Chase, then at Jason as he continued. "It's all right, Dad. We know you miss Mom. I guess we all understand that."

"I'm sorry." Jason nodded. "No, I really am sorry. I had no idea...well, I guess I did, but I didn't know that you boys had come to think that it was you I didn't want to be here for."

"Dad, you tell us every time you see us that you hate being around. I don't know what else you could have us do. We love you." Dad nodded and stood up. "I wish that I could tell you that we understand, but to be honest, I don't. Having you here, all the time, it's been a wonderful life. But it makes us all feel bad when all you want to do is leave. If having a mate can make you feel this way, I certainly don't want one in my life. That's the way I've felt for decades."

"It's not, I promise you. And as for bitching, I won't. Not anymore. I might slip up but.... I'm truly sorry about that. I am. And I'm going to be better at it. I swear it." Chase nodded and hugged his dad. "Thank you. I should have...I'm not saying that you should have told me sooner, because I'm not sure I would have listened, but I'm going to be a better father and man for you. I might even stop calling you boys."

"That would be great."

They were all three laughing as they made their way out of the conference room and to the main lobby. Chase wondered how long it would be before Dad started to complain once more, and decided that he'd not mention it to him again when he did. He hadn't meant to hurt his dad so badly.

~~~

Jason worked on his notes all the way to the steakhouse.

He was sure that he was missing a few points and that he was going to come off as a bastard, but if they wanted to continue to be in business, then changes were going to have to be made. And he was good at being a prick.

It hadn't been his intention to become the heavy in the business world. Jason, he thought, was the most laid back of all of his brothers. But not lately. He was short with people, avoided contact with most of his family, and he was keeping busy with getting his house in order. He supposed they were all excuses, but he liked his own company and didn't care if it pissed people off.

"I have four emails from a man by the name of Spencer Graham. Do you know him?" Jason told Chase that he didn't. "Me either. They're just notes, really, that say that he would like to talk to us about a business deal. He said that he's got an idea that will make us millions."

"Sure he does. Everyone has ideas that'll make them a million, but not the investor. Just tell him that we'll get back to him sometime in the future." Chase nodded and said he'd do it now. "Did you know that Canada Pans had nearly seven hundred employees at one time? That was only as recently as five years ago. Now they're down to a couple hundred. That's a big dump."

"They should have done it years ago, but with the last sales report and taxes, he had to do something." Jason nodded. "I think, if I can get him to do this, he would be able to hire that many back, plus a lot more if he wants. This could really bring him out of the red."

"I'm working on that now."

As soon as they were at the restaurant, he put his computer away. So did Chase. They wouldn't discuss work

19

at the dinner table if they were with family. It didn't matter if it was just two of them or all, no business at the table. His dad had taught them that.

Jason thought about his dad as they made their way to the table. He had been really hurt about what he'd said to him. And in turn it had hurt Jason as well. His dad hadn't made it easy on them for the past few hundred years.

Dinner was just the way he liked it…shouting over each other to make a point on something as mundane as what their favorite ice cream was. Vanilla was his, and highly underrated. There was a heated debate about which baseball team was going to win this year. And his personal favorite, where to eat dessert. His family was the best, if not a little too much at times.

His cell was ringing and he let it go to voicemail. He knew it was something to do with work and didn't want to deal with it, even after they were done there.

After having ice cream cones with his family, Jason opted to head home rather than go to the movies with them. He was exhausted and knew it was coming up on him needing to feed. He thought that might be what was making him so cranky, but didn't know. Once he found someone that he could feed from, he would feel a little better. Going home, he looked at his cell before plugging it in. There were ten messages, four text messages, as well as several emails. Ignoring them in favor of sleep, he stripped down and fell on his bed. Jason was asleep before his head hit the pillow.

Waking to the sound of his doorbell ringing, he got up to go and answer it. Fuck this shit. Whoever this was they might be his next fucking meal. Tearing the door open before Garrett could answer it for him, he looked at the figure standing in the dark.

"What the fuck do you want? Do you have any clue as to what time it is?" Garrett cleared his throat and looked at him. Jason was naked and just didn't care. Looking back at the soaking wet person at the door, he asked them again.

"Yes, I'm well aware of what time it is, you moronic fuck. Where the hell is your robe?" He didn't even bother covering himself when he realized the figure was a woman. "Can you put that thing away before you poke someone's eye out with it?"

"Are you going to be down between my legs for me to do that?" She threw back the hood on her jacket and punched him. Jason fell back to the floor and hit his head on the table behind him. "What the fuck was that for?"

"You just propositioned me. I do not go down on men just because they have an impressive dick. The one between your legs, not the one you think with." A blanket was tossed to him from Garrett and he covered himself with it. "Where is Jason Crosby? I'm here to talk to his ass."

"His ass, my lady, is on the floor." She looked at Garrett when he spoke, then at him. Jason felt his cock ache, his body respond to the goddess in front of him when she took off her sopping wet jacket. "Would you care for some tea, my lady? Or perhaps something stronger?"

"Whiskey, if you have it." Garrett nodded and looked at him. "He'll take what I'm having, or he can do without. He's made me wait long enough."

"Do I know you?" She put out her hand. "Are you thinking that I should trust you now to lift me up without causing me more damage? I don't think so."

Jason stood and was surprised that she was almost as tall

21

as his six foot four frame. And she was strong too. Her right arm was covered in a tattoo that he thought went from the back of her hand to up under her shirt. There were hints of it on her shoulder and neck, but he was afraid to ask her if he could see it. She might hit him again. And once was more than enough.

When Garrett returned, he had a short glass of whiskey for them both, and a pair of pants for him. Dropping the blanket to pull on his pants, he laughed when she turned her back to him. This was a distraction that he might enjoy.

"My name is Spencer Graham. I've been trying to reach you for a week now." He remembered the name, but not what she'd been trying to contact him about. "I have an idea I want to talk to you about. And I'm here at four in the morning because we have until nine-thirty this morning, thanks to you, to act upon it."

"And why would I care to go into business with you? I have no idea who you are. What you're about. Nor do I have a single clue why I'm even entertaining the idea of speaking to you." He watched her walk away and into his study. Garrett cleared his throat and he looked at him. "You know something about this?"

"Yes, I told her to go to your office in the morning. Well, today. She said it was hard to get past your barracuda that you have working the front desk. I'm assuming that she means Ms. Curtain. I told you she was a terror." He nodded and looked when Ms. Graham yelled for him to get his ass in there. "She has a way about herself, doesn't she, sir?"

"Yes, she does. And quite lovely too. Call my brother Grayson in, would you? If I have to listen to her, so does he. He's the man that gets things done." Garrett started away and Jason remembered something else. "My dad. Call him as well. He said at dinner tonight that he wanted to be more involved in things."

"Very good, sir."

When Garrett was gone, Jason moved to the study. Ms. Graham was making herself at home, it appeared, and was lying on his couch. When he walked closer to her, he found her reading a report that had been on his desk for a week now.

"What do you think you're doing?" He tried to snatch it from her but she moved before he could. "That does not belong to you. And if this is your way of getting my help, you're failing badly."

"You said you didn't know me, yet here is a report that I sent you over a month ago." He didn't even try to deny it, simply because he didn't know what it said...he'd never read it. "What the fuck were you going to do, take this from me?"

Jason needed to cool his temper. So instead of getting into another argument with her, he moved to his desk and sat down. He looked at her, trying to equate his mind around the fact that she'd hit him. It hadn't hurt, but she'd hit him.

"My brother, Grayson, is coming here. He'll know more about this than me." She snorted at him and he had to count to ten. "It's four in the morning and here you are at my doorstep making demands on me. The very least you could do is be polite."

He took a healthy drink of his whiskey and swallowed hard around it. Jason stretched his neck and heard it pop. He was sure that she had as well. While she sipped from her glass, he looked at her. Christ, she was more than just lovely, she was sexy as hell.

"You're not human." He said that he was not. "I might

have known that, but didn't really care. It's your money that I need, not whatever you are. So long as you don't go on some sort of tasting spree with my neck, then you could be Jack the Ripper for all I give a shit."

"Money. It always comes down to the almighty buck, doesn't it? And how much did you think to take me for?" He watched her face and loved how she angered prettily. "Again, it's four in the morning, I have a right to be snarky."

"I don't know. I have a feeling that you're in a constant state of snarky. Not only that, but I'm betting you're a know-it-all, a jerk, and an all-around jackass. I need just under four hundred thousand. If you had bothered to look at this report, you would have known that as well. The building is going cheap, but the cost will come into retooling it for what I have in mind. It will employ just under two thousand people when it's fully operational. And it will give job opportunities around the community as well. Jobs will bring in an influx of money, which will help the schools, the library, as well as things like restaurants and medical personnel."

Grayson and his dad walked in just as he was asking for the paperwork. As he looked it over, he not only saw that there was a prospectus on what the money would go for, but also a sheet on timelines of the building's retooling, as she called it, and what the project would entail.

She was bringing the other two up to speed while he read over the letter she had sent him. Then he pulled up the emails from the last few days, also from her. Those were more polite than she'd been in person, and he wondered if she'd had someone write them for her. No, he decided, she'd do this, just because she'd not trust someone else to work for her.

"You wish to manufacture gift bags." She nodded and

handed him a thick envelope that was filled with samples. "These are lovely, but what sort of market are you planning to hit with these? For a buck, I could go to the store and get a package of them. What makes yours so special?"

"Bags are easy and cheap to use. They're also a product that goes into the landfill when they're used up. These are not only biodegradable, but they also have seeds embedded into them that will sprout flowers or herbs when they're done. Just take them in the backyard, cover them with a little soil, and you have flowers." He liked that idea and said so. "Well, that must have hurt. You giving out a compliment. Do you do that often?"

"No, he doesn't." Grayson winked at the woman and continued. "This planting thing. What if the bag gets wet? I mean, the gift might have a little moisture on it, or there might be a rainstorm while going to little Tommy's birthday party. What then?"

She pulled the sheets from Jason and handed them to Grayson. "This is a sheet of conventional waxed paper. It's coated with paraffin wax. We don't use that. Ours is made from soybean. Which is clean, safe, non-toxic, and biodegradable. It's also from a renewable and sustainable resource." She handed him the second sheet, and he could feel the difference immediately. "The company that makes this product is willing to help out with the costs of using this if we tag his company name in the finished product."

"And the reason we're here at this time of the morning?" Dad looked at Jason, then back at Spencer as he continued. "Not that I mind being pulled from my bed to see a pretty woman, but this could have waited, I think."

"There was plenty of time when I first approached you,

but that's all gone now. The building that I want to buy, with your help, is going to auction at nine-thirty this morning. I've been trying to get in touch with your company for weeks now. It's going to go cheap, but even at that, I don't have the resources to purchase it right now. That's why I'm here." She looked at him. "I can't purchase it and start this venture without financial assistance."

CHAPTER 2

Spencer didn't like the man. Not one bit. He was sexy as fuck, tall, and well built. He also had an impressive cock. But he was also arrogant, snobbish, and a bastard. And right now, if someone were to hand her a gun, she was sure that she'd gladly go to the chair for killing him. She glanced at her watch again.

"You know, I can tell what time it is." She'd wanted to bash his head in every minute since they'd come here. "We have plenty of time."

"It's ten minutes after nine. That is not plenty of time." He nodded and kept walking the length of the building. She wondered if he was going to take dust samples next, or have the windows measured for curtains. "If we're not there to bid, then I'm going to murder you in your sleep."

"It takes a very powerful person to do that. I've been taken care of. What do you plan to do for bay docking? There is no room for them to come in on this side of the building." She turned him to the other end of the place. "Ah. I must have missed them."

"I don't know how. You've been over this place like it's got some hidden treasure, and you're going to find it or know the reason why. It's fifteen minutes after." He nodded again.

"You are fucking driving me crazy. Why do you have to do this right this minute?"

"Because when I invest my money in something, I want to know what I'm getting." He looked her up and down, and Spencer felt her body heat up. Not in an embarrassed sort of way, either. He pulled out his cell and made a call. "Dad, go ahead and register us for the bidding, we'll be there in five minutes."

"You had someone there? All this time? Why didn't you tell me?" He asked her what fun that would have been. "Christ, I hope after today I don't have to deal with you much. You're too much to have to talk to all the time. If I do, then one of us isn't going to come out without a long prison term. Me, most likely."

"If this deal goes through, you'll deal with all of us. We each have a different part in every deal we take on." They were headed to his car when he turned and looked at the front of the building. "This isn't going to be able to house you in a few years. Why this one? You have to know that there are bigger ones all over this area."

"My father helped build it." He watched her, and she didn't squirm like she normally did when someone looked at her like he was. "You should get in. I'll meet you there."

"No, ride with me. I have questions." She said of course you do, and he laughed. Spencer felt it like a gentle caress on her skin, and that made her snappish. Telling him no, she headed to her own car. "I would like to ask you questions, Ms. Graham. Or I don't buy it."

"You fucking bastard." He told her he'd been called worse. "I just bet you have, and I'm betting by your own family too."

"If you please?" When he held the door open for her, she

wanted to go to the other side and slide in, but she needed him and his money so she got in. But she wasn't going to be impressed with the ride. She'd let him think that riding in a limo was something she did with regularity. "What do you know of shifters and vampires?"

"Know of them? Nothing. I mean, I've met a few, but I don't socialize with them, if that's what you're asking me. I don't have anything against them, I just don't socialize at all if I can help it." He nodded. "Which are you?"

"Vampire." She looked out the window then back at him. "Long ago we saved some faeries from a burning building. And in return for us saving them, the queen gave us a gift. The gift of sunlight. In addition to a few other perks. But all in all, we can function and live as humans forever. And we're safe from things like stakes and other magic meant to kill us."

"Okay, that explains a lot, but why do you think I'd care? I already told you, so long as we can work together, you could be anything you wanted. But I will add, there will be no snacking on my neck. I don't care if someone, and I'm sure there is a line of them somewhere, wants to tear your throat out for you just being you." He nodded. then looked out the window with an odd look on his face. "I'd like to know when you get the building and when we can start on construction."

"As soon as you come to understand something about us." She told him there was no us. "There is, I'm afraid. You're my mate. My other half. Whatever you call it, you belong to me. And, with that being said, we —"

"I don't belong to anyone, you asshat. I'm an adult and have a mind of my own. And belonging to you would be a kind of hell that I don't even want to contemplate. Not now or ever." He nodded. "How do you even know that this isn't a

29

fluke or something? Maybe you can't find a date or whatever, and you decided that I might be a good time. I won't be, let me tell you that right now. I don't even like you."

"I don't care all that much for you either, if we're being truthful. But the fact remains, you belong to me." She wanted to hit him. Maybe even stake him a time or two. But she just sat there, wondering now how she was going to get out of this arrangement with him.

"I want you to call your dad and tell him I've changed my mind. I'm not going into business with you." Jason just leaned back in his seat and stared at her. "I'm not going to be anything to you, not for any kind of money. I'd rather fail at this than have to be subjected to you for the rest of my days. And when you say that I belong to you? Well, that just curls up in my belly so badly that I want to spew puke all over your nice fancy clothing."

"It's too late for that." She didn't even bother speaking to him the rest of the trip. He did ask about the building and the product, but since she wasn't going to work with him, Spencer thought it wasn't any of his business. As soon as they stopped, she was ready to leap from the vehicle when he grabbed her arm. "What do you think this is going to prove? Stop being childish and listen to me."

"Fuck you." She jerked from his grip and fell out of the car. As soon as she was on her feet, she went inside. It hadn't been her plan to go, but she figured that she was safer with people around. And by the looks of it, there were a lot of them around today.

Mr. Crosby was sitting in the front row. When he saw her, he waved for her to come to him. There was about two minutes before the bidding started, and she had plenty of time

30

to tell him she'd changed her mind. As she made her way up front, she thought of all the things she'd been planning to do with the money. Buying her dad a marker for his grave would have to wait.

"I'm not going to go into business with you guys. I'm sorry to have wasted your time." He looked to her left, and she knew that Jack Turd was right behind her. "Thank you so much for your time, and I'm sorry again about waking you at such an ungodly hour."

She straightened up to leave and was grabbed on the arm again. Spencer doubled up her fist and turned to hit Asshat again when she was shoved into a seat. Before she could stand up and leave, he put his hand on her leg and told her not to move. Right then Spencer could have easily screamed her head off, but didn't want to embarrass herself. Not to mention, she was sort of afraid of the bigger man. He leaned over her so that his throat was right at her hand, and she had to double her fist so as not to grab him and hurt him.

"Dad, Spencer is my mate. And she's as pissed about it as I am." Mr. Crosby looked at him then at her. "She'd rather lose out on this opportunity than to be with me. And since I have no intentions of leaving a good investment to die, she's going to have to deal with it, and her belonging to me."

"I see. Actually, no I don't, but then, I'm still trying to get over you ordering her about like she's a toddler." Spencer sat still, but she wasn't going to be there for very long. As soon as he removed his hand from her, or she did it permanently, she was out of there. Mr. Crosby patted her on the leg and whispered in her ear. "There, my dear. Just sit tight and we'll get this settled out. You're going to be a hell of an addition to this family."

31

"No, I will not." She fought the tears that filled her eyes. Nothing ever seemed to go her way, ever. And when the auctioneer said it was time, she closed off her mind to everything but her thoughts. But she did turn to Mr. Crosby again. "Don't bid. I wouldn't take money from him if he was the last man on earth and I was dying of hunger. I don't like him. And if you have to buy it because he's an asshole, then I won't work with you. You'll have this building for nothing."

He nodded but said nothing. The first building up for bid wasn't the one that she had wanted, so she ignored it. All she could think about was him telling her that he didn't want her. And that she belonged to him. Belonged to him like she was something that he could put on a shelf or stuff in a closet.

She supposed it should have been all right, she didn't want anything to do with him either. But he'd been such an asshole about it. Spencer would bet that was how he did everything, with an iron fist and never a kind word. As the bidding war went on around her, she thought of her dad.

He'd been such a kind and gentle man. All her life she'd never heard him say a harsh word to anyone, nor did he raise his voice. The one and only time she'd seen him upset was just after they told him he only had months to live, and she'd said she was coming home to stay with him.

"You will stay at college until you're finished. I'll be here for you when you've done this." She had worried and fretted over him so much that he'd finally come to see her on campus, showing her, she figured, that he was still capable of getting around without her help. After that, school was easier. And her grades, which had slipped just a bit, improved with less worry.

Then eight days after she got her degree, he'd gone into

JASON

a store and been shot. Like he was nothing at all to someone. Spencer missed him more every day. And now she'd failed him and his legacy to her. The insurance money that he'd left her was to build a name for herself. All she'd managed to do with it was make a few mockups for an already failed business.

At ten till noon, the family stood up. Spencer knew they were going to lunch, but wasn't going to join them. She had a few bucks and would eat here rather than go out with them. As she stood in line to order herself a cold drink, one of the brothers came to stand by her.

"Sean." She nodded and moved forward when the line did. "I'm to ask you politely if you'd like to join us. If not, then I'm to stay with you in case you try to run off."

"I can 'run off,' as you put it, if I want to. And if Asswipe is ordering you around too, I want you to realize that you wear big boy panties too and should tell him to fuck off. Not that it does any good, but you should tell him that. Maybe he'd back off a bit." He nodded and grinned at her. "You think you're charming, don't you?"

"I am. You're just seeing me on an off day. My dad likes you, by the way." She didn't say anything. "I guess you don't care for Jason. I'm sorry about that. I don't know when he became such a stick in the mud. But over the last few decades he's become more and more.... What you called him. An asswipe."

"Call it like it is, Sean. He's an overbearing prick that thinks his way is the only way." Sean laughed, and she did find herself charmed by him, just a little. "I'm not going to go into business with your family. I don't know why you've been sent to watch-dog me. Last I knew, I was a grown woman that

33

could come and go as I pleased. But he has it in his head that I belong to him. And I belong to no one but myself."

"You could run, but he'd just find you. He can, you know. Jason has your scent." She knew that as well. "Besides, you're not hard on the eyes, and the fact that you have Jason all twisted up like a vine makes me like you too. He's tough on people."

"No shit. It's because he's the all-powerful Jason Crosby and people should bow before him." Sean laughed again. "I'm going to have a drink. Would you like one?"

"Yes, please. Just a water." She ordered them both a water and they sat at the picnic tables outside that had been there since she could remember. "You said that you no longer wanted to go into business with us. Is it because of Jason?"

"Yes." She drank her water and looked around. Tomorrow they'd auction off pigs and cattle here, and there were already trucks lined up to bring in their wares. "When I was a little girl, my dad used to bring me here to the auctions. We never bought any of the animals, but we'd come to see them. It was cheaper than the zoo, and no one cared if I got up close and personal with them, nor did they care that I got dirty. I guess that was the most appealing thing for me. Being able to get as dirty as I wanted. And to be closer to something that other kids my age never got to see. My dad took me to a lot of places like this. I've only come to realize since he died that it was because we were broke all the time."

"I bet you didn't get all that dirty, did you?" She looked at Sean and smiled. "Yeah, I thought so. You have a look about you that says, while you don't care what you look like, you aren't dirty or mussy. My dad is like that too. He could be in his holey jeans and an old tee shirt, and so long as they were clean and he was, he wouldn't care. Nor does he care what people think about him. He's a good man."

"He seems to be. All of you do. You don't have to be nice to me, Sean. I'm not going to run. I might later, but for now, I'm going to see how much somebody else pays for the building." He said nothing. "I'm sorry you got the short straw and had to stay here, missing your lunch."

"Trust me, it's been no hardship staying with you. In fact, all of us wanted to stay with you. I was lucky." She nodded. "You don't believe me, do you? I'm telling you the truth. Once my dad made it clear that you were Jason's mate, we all wanted to jump at the chance to get to know you. I won."

She started crying then. He was so nice to her that it hurt. And when he came to sit next to her on the same side of the bench she was on, she let him hold her. No one had done that in a very long time.

~~~

Sean wasn't sure what had upset her, but he had a feeling that it was Jason. He'd been a bear of late, but making his mate cry wasn't going to slide by him. Sean might be the youngest, but he knew more about women than any of his brothers did. He studied them. Quite extensively, as a matter of fact.

He held her until she seemed to get some control over herself. Then he offered her two of the napkins that had come with their drinks. She wiped at her eyes and cheeks but said nothing. Sean tried to think what he could say to her that would make her feel better.

"My dad, he has been in a funk for a while." She told him she wasn't in a funk. "I know that. I was only saying he was. You see, we have this ability to stay in the sunlight. Which means that he can no longer meet the sun to go to Mom. I

35

think for a while there, I was avoiding him because he was telling us how he'd been lied to by the queen when she gave us this gift. Every time we saw him. I don't think he realized how much he was telling us that. But today...I've never seen him in such a good mood. He really likes you."

"I like him too. He's a good man, and for the most part, raised some good men. It's been hard on me too, I guess. My dad died a few years ago, but I would never have avoided him." Sean told her he was sorry, he'd not meant to be so crass. "I'm sorry too. I'm also sorry that your dad is missing his wife so much. I miss my dad a great deal."

"Anyway, Dad had it in his head, like I said, that he was ripped off. So yesterday, before going to dinner with the family, someone said something to him about it." She asked if it was Jason. "No, this time it was Chase. But any of us might have said it, it was becoming that bad to be around him. Every time something was mentioned, he would talk about how he couldn't see Mom. I think we were all feeling like he didn't want to be with us. It hurt us, me too, that he was so set to leave us that it felt as if he didn't want to be around us. And vice versa too."

"Maybe he didn't think you guys wanted to be with him. Perhaps he was feeling useless, and decided that joining your mom was better than hanging around you guys." He'd not thought of it that way and told her that. "He's a nice man, your father. I can't believe he's the father of Asshat."

"Asshat, huh? Sounds like a good name for him. But I won't call him that. Not to his face, anyway. He's hard enough to be around." She laughed. "Okay, it's about time we go back. Would you share nachos and cheese with me? And one of those pretzels?"

Sean wasn't hungry. So when she told him no thanks, he was sort of grateful for it. He'd fed last night, and it would be a while before he wanted not just food, but blood either. But he knew if she was going to be dealing with Jason, she'd need every drop of her strength. Neither of them was going to come into this easily. And he was going to enjoy watching his brother come to terms with this firecracker. But he was going to keep an eye on her. She wasn't fragile, but she had enough hurt in her life, and didn't need Jason mucking it up more.

They sat down before his family came back. He thought it was funny to watch Jason around Spencer. She had placed herself on the end of the row and him on the other side of her. Jason asked him to move, but Spencer told Jason that if he sat next to her, she would hurt him. Sean had a feeling it wasn't an idle threat either. Apparently neither did Jason. He sat as far from her as he could and still be in the same row.

Sean was in the middle of something big, both literally and figuratively. He knew that if Jason had wanted to, he could have ordered him to move and he would have had no choice in the matter. And he didn't tell her this, but Spencer wasn't able to hurt Jason. At least he didn't think so. But they were going to be hard on each other. And he was sure that it was going to be his brother who lost this one. That didn't mean he wasn't going to keep an eye on her as well.

The bidding wasn't nearly as boring as he thought it would be. Watching the faces of the people bidding on buildings and other equipment that the city was trying to unload was interesting. He could tell when someone was as close to their limit as they were going to go. The enjoyment on someone's face that won what they wanted, and the disappointment on the faces of those that lost. Sean wondered if Spencer's dad

37

had enjoyed this part of the day with his daughter too.

He didn't have to know when the building that she was interested in came up. Spencer grew stiff, her hands clenched in her lap. Sean glanced at his brother and saw him doing the same. Jason would buy the building if for no other reason than she didn't want him to. There was going to be a lot of hell to be played out before these two got together.

The bidding, like with the other buildings, started out much higher than anyone would pay for it. He'd done his homework on the place when asked by Jason, and he knew just what was wrong with the building. What it needed in repairs, as well as how long it had been sitting empty. Jason would make a sound bid, but he had a feeling it wasn't going to be the right one. Spencer was set to kill him anyway, and this wouldn't help.

"The building is only worth about twenty grand. If Asshat pays more than that for it, because I know as well as you that he's going to buy it, then he's a bigger fool than I thought he was." Sean glanced at his brother when he felt his eyes looking at him. "He's thinking he's all bad assed by staring at me. Well, I don't care. He's an idiot if he thinks I'm going to mind him like a five-year-old."

"He can hear you, you know that, don't you?" She nodded. "Okay then. Would you mind not putting me between the two of you? I don't mind watching, but I don't want to get hurt when you hit him."

"He's going to do it, isn't he?" Her voice was much lower, but Sean knew that Jason could still hear her. "Just because I told him no, he's going to show me by buying it anyway. Because he's some macho shit that has to have the last word. And even though he knows that I no longer wish to do business with him or his family, he'll do that anyway as well, just because he thinks he knows more than anyone else."

She didn't say another word for the rest of the auction. Not when Jason won the bid at ten thousand dollars, nor when she was told that it was going to be in her name. Sean felt bad for her. She'd only wanted to do something for herself, build herself a business, and Jason had soured it for her.

It was well after five when they were ready to leave. She didn't ask for a ride; Sean thought it was just assumed that she'd ride with them to the restaurant to celebrate. When he was standing by the car with the rest of them, waiting for her to come out, Jason came to stand next to him.

"Don't." Jason asked him what he meant. "Don't ask me about her. Don't bother me with details about how you're going to tame her. And I most certainly don't want you to tell me that she's being childish again. What you did in there and to her was wrong and you know it."

"She is being childish. To think that we got the building for a great deal less than she thought, I thought she'd be thrilled." Sean said nothing. "You have to admit, it was a better deal than you said I'd get."

"Yes, it was. But at what cost to her?" Sean walked away. Not too far...he was going to make sure that Spencer was all right before he left. But he was over with spending time with Jason today.

Ten minutes later, he saw his dad come out of the building. He was smiling, so that could only mean that he'd found someone he knew or something had happened with Spencer. He hoped that she had left Jason standing there with his head up his ass.

Jason looked at the front of the building, then at his watch,

39

something Sean had only just realized that his brother did a great deal. Like he didn't have forever to get to someplace, to make his own way in the world, but everything had to be set to a timeframe that he had. Jason really was an asshat.

"Where is she? We have reservations at seven. And while I know that they'll hold our table, I don't want to be late for this because she has a burr up her ass." Dad asked Jason who he was talking about. "Damn it, Dad. Spencer. Where the hell is she?"

"Did you ask her to come to dinner with us?" Jason said no, but they had talked about it. "You and I talked about it. Sean and Grayson talked about it. I didn't hear her say a word, did you guys?"

Sean watched his brothers shake their heads. They were enjoying this too. Watching someone like little human Spencer take on Jason and not give a shit who he was. It was funny to watch Jason try to tame the one woman that Sean knew wouldn't take his shit.

"She's pissing me off." Dad laughed and Sean did as well. "What do you find so funny about all this? That my mate is out there someplace and I don't have a clue as to where? Do you want her to get hurt or worse, get herself into something that gets her killed?"

Sean shrugged and decided to defend his new friend. "I'm reasonably sure that she's stronger and smarter than you've given her credit for. And if trouble finds her, I'm sure that she can get herself out of it. And if she can't, she's smart enough to know to call in help. However, I'd not count on that being you. Not the way you treat her. By the way, did you not taste her? Well, I can guess why not. She might have ripped your head off had you tried." Jason growled at him. "You can be

40

pissy all you want, but you are only getting what you deserve with her. To think that she had you pegged so well makes me as happy as I've been in a while. I'm betting right now you're wondering what sort of ropes to use on her to keep her in line. That's what you're planning, isn't it, Jason, to keep her in line?"

"This is none of your fucking business." It wasn't, and he nodded that Jason was right. "Where is she? You know. You were all cozy with her all afternoon. Sitting over there with your heads all close. Don't think I didn't notice, nor hear what you had to say about me."

"Then you'll know that I told her you could hear her and her saying she didn't care. As for where she is, I don't know. And if I did know, I don't think I'd tell you." Jason stepped closer to him, his face hard in anger. "Hit me and I'll hurt you in ways you'll never heal from. As was pointed out to me today, I'm wearing big boy panties and I'm not going to be your whipping dog in this. Not this time."

"That's enough." Dad stepped between them and Sean backed away. He was going to take a walk, as far from Jason as he could get, when his dad said his name. "Where is she, Sean? She won't be hurt, will she?"

"I don't know where she is, Dad. But I don't think anyone will hurt her any more than Jason did, and will continue to do if he finds her." Jason asked him what the fuck that meant, but Sean was talking to his dad, not him, right now. "We talked about her dad and the building, nothing more. And she wasn't happy that her dreams were shattered today. Nor her heart. She cried on my shoulder today because I was nice to her. That's all, just because I was nice to her."

Sean left them there. He didn't know who he was more

41

upset with...Jason, who had treated her so badly, or himself for not making sure that she was going to be all right. As he made his way to his home, he thought of the look on her face when she talked about her dad.

Love. It was almost tangible. She loved the man, and his love for her shone all over her. As he made his way into his house, he thought of where she might be and decided to look her up. Her father's home, and he'd bet anything she was living there all alone.

JASON

CHAPTER 3

Spencer was sitting at her desk, just staring off into space, when Sean saw her in the window. Getting up, she made her way to him, pulling her sweater tighter around her. It wasn't cold, not in mid-July, but she seemed to need it, the comfort of it wrapped around her.

"Hi. You know, it was harder than I thought to find you." Stunned, he'd bet, that he'd even want to find her, she looked around. "Jason isn't here. He has no idea that I am. I won't tell him either."

"Why?" Sean asked her what she meant. "Why were you trying to find me, and why would he even care if you're here or not? It's not like we're going to be anything to each other. He's a bastard."

"Yes, he is, but I wanted to make sure you were all right. I meant to come by last night, but I didn't figure out the name on the property here until early this morning. By then it was too late." He grinned. "I'm babbling. May I be invited in? I'm not sure if you know this or not, but you have to invite a vampire in. Also, just in case you might need to know this, you can put stipulations on the visit too. Like saying this one time I can come in, but I have to be invited again. Just in case."

"You mean your brother. All right. I like that. Would

43

you like to come in, Sean?" He nodded and stepped over the threshold. He stood there for several seconds. "What's wrong?"

"Sorrow. There is a great deal of sorrow in this house." He looked at her and she didn't say anything. "I'm sorry. You loved him very much, didn't you? I mean, I knew that…you show it every time you talk about him. But you're grieving more than just a little. I'm terribly sorry for your loss. If I can—"

"Don't. Not today." He nodded. "I was just going to have a cup of tea. Would you like some? If not, I have coffee, but it's not fresh. Nor expensive. Dad didn't care for the good stuff. And to be honest, I never did learn to make it. He said that…. Now I'm babbling."

"Juice if you have it. If not, tea is fine." She said she had juice. He followed her to the kitchen and had to smile. "You cook. And well too, I would imagine."

"I like to play in the kitchen, if that's what you mean. The herbs were here for my dad to use, and I never had the heart to get rid of them." He touched his fingers to the line of herbs that were in a long groove in the middle of the table. "I find that I use them in things now. Not as much as Dad did, but I love the smell of them when cooking. And I discovered I have a taste for garlic. I don't suppose that matters to you guys either."

"No, sorry, it's a myth. I particularly love the smell of fresh rosemary and thyme. Those are my favorites." She nodded and handed him a large glass of orange juice. "I want to be your friend, Spencer. I think that you were treated poorly by my brother, and it wasn't right of him. But I do want you to think of me as a friend. And I promise you that whatever we talk about, I won't go and tell him any of it."

"I don't know how to be a friend, Sean. I mean, I don't have many. A few acquaintances, a couple of people that I used to work with, but not anyone that I would call up and ask to have lunch with me." He nodded as if he understood. "My dad, he was my friend. I know people would say that I've hung onto his memories and his death for too long, but he was all I had in this world, and some dick decided that robbing the store he was in and killing him was just a part of his day. His two second decision took away my reason for living for a very long time."

"I'm so sorry, Spencer." He laughed a little. "When I was searching for your home, I was looking for someone with the name of Graham. There was no one, not a single person, in this entire town with that last name that owns any sort of property or rents anything. Then I put in Spencer — in desperation, mind you — and got a hit. Your mom, she had this house before she married your dad. This is the Spencer house."

"Yes. I was named after her. I didn't know her at all. She died right after I was born. Complications, Dad told me. Anyway, he raised me all on his own and we had fun. Not a lot of money, but fun." Sean sipped his juice, afraid that she'd ask him to leave if he was finished with it. While he watched her, she pulled out a tiny roast and put it in a cast iron skillet to brown. "We did things that most little girls wouldn't even think of. Fishing. We loved to do that. As I got older, it occurred to me that it wasn't only the fun we were having doing that, but that we were getting us some meat for dinner. I didn't realize just how broke we were until much later, as I said. But he made sure that we did things all the

45

time while we traveled around. And that we ate a good meal when we had it."

"Tell me how you came up with the bag idea." She asked him why. "Because I'm curious. You have a good head on your shoulders, and I'm betting that this isn't your only idea to make some money."

"No. I was always dreaming of better ways to make the world a better place." She took one potato from the bowl that looked like it had been there too long. But she peeled it, cutting away the bad parts, and then put it in the pan with the roast. "I make purses from plastic grocery bags. They sell well on the internet, by the way. I take old blankets that have too many holes in them to be considered any kind of covering, and make them into teddy bears and other animals. Those I donate to the local hospital. The kids get one when they leave. Just things that reuse what we have thrown out and make it useful again. Dad and I—again with my dad—when we'd take walks, we had a bag with us to pick up trash and other things that people would just discard. Like this earth is their own personal dumping ground."

"I've seen that too. When you live as long as we do, you see things that you would never have thought a person would do. Like littering. You're a nice person, Spencer Graham." She smiled at him as a single carrot was peeled and cut up. He noticed that there were only two more in the fridge, along with a quart of milk, a carton of eggs, and some containers that had come from a restaurant, he'd bet. "Are you making enough money?"

"No, I'm not." She looked at him. "This is the last meat that I'll have for a while. And the veggies that are in my garden didn't do so well. I think that the neighbor is taking them, but if they need food that badly, then they can have it. Milk isn't expensive, but I've been cutting back on it as well. When I lost my job about four months ago they promised me unemployment, but they didn't allow it when it came to putting the paperwork through. Downsizing is a bitch."

"Do you need any?" She shook her head and told him she'd find something soon. "I know, but you might need some bread or something. Let me give you some money. I'd feel better if you did."

"I'm not telling you this because I want you to feel any way toward me. I'm broke...more than broke, but that's all right too. This house is paid for, thank goodness, and the taxes are all paid up for the next five years. If I can't find a job in that amount of time, then I'm better off living on the streets." He hurt that she was so destitute. "It's fine. I promise you. I have two job interviews in the morning, and if that doesn't work out, I can always take on male clients to meet the bills."

"No." She laughed and he felt his face heat up. "You were joking. I'm sorry. The thought of you.... Never mind. But you have to promise me, if you need anything, you let me know."

She never promised him, and he was sort of sorry that she'd not. Instead, she invited him to have dinner with her, and he, of course, declined. But he was going to do something for her. He had no idea what it would be, but he'd find a way to help her. As he was leaving, he thought of something else and looked around the house. It occurred to him then how much she'd been willing to put forth to make her idea work.

"You sold off your furniture." She nodded. "To make the prototypes. What else did you do to make the money?"

"Not prostitution, if that's what you're asking." He said he wasn't. "I used my dad's insurance money. He told me to, to live on for him. I really wanted it to work. I had plans for a little of that money, but I can get it eventually."

Sean did something he knew he would regret and looked into her mind. It was there. The disappointment of not being able to afford a headstone for her dad. The fact that she might lose the house in six months due to the city making demands on her property that she couldn't afford. New sewer and hidden electrical lines. And the cable company wanted to dig in her yard to put lines to their other customers, and were fighting her for the rights to just do it. Not that they'd do it for free—nothing was free—but they'd charge her for the equipment as well as the lines that would run over her land.

"Can I come back? I'd like to see you, and to develop our friendship." She told him as long as he came alone, she was fine with it. "I will. I promise. And, Spencer, you will be all right. You know that, don't you?"

"Of course I do."

She left him there, tears in her eyes, and closed the door. He hurt, more than he ever had, even when his mom had passed away. Sean decided to go to see his brother.

~~~

Jason was going over the building again when he saw Sean coming toward him. Good, he needed a fresh set of eyes. But before he could comment on what he needed from him, he found himself flat on his back and looking up at a very pissed off face.

"I'm sure that you have a very good explanation for this. What the fuck was that for?" Sean just stood over him, telling him to get up. "Are you planning to hit me again? If so, then no, I'll stay right here."

The kick to his ribs hurt, and Jason felt two of them snap

under the pressure. He tried to roll away from the abuse, but Sean was faster and seemed to not care at all that he was hurting him badly. Finally, having enough, Jason stood up and fought back. In minutes, they were both bloodied with broken bones. Dad stopped them just as Sean was coming at him again.

"What the fuck is wrong with you two?" Sean said it was his fault. "What did you do now, Jason?"

"Me? I was working and he comes out of nowhere and proceeds to beat the shit out of me." Sean said he wasn't finished either. "I don't have any idea what provoked him into this rage. I wasn't even near him all morning. And apparently that's all it takes for someone to want to cause me harm, just for me being around them. You people need to back the—"

"You left her to fail." Jason just knew this was going to be about that woman again. "Did you know that she sank every penny she had, and some that she didn't, into making her idea work? And what do you do? You humiliate her, treat her like a subhuman, and then walk all over her feelings. Christ, Jason, you can be a bastard to us all you need to, but she's your mate. The woman that will be there for you no matter how things go. Not that such things matter to you, I guess. You're Jason Crosby, king of the bastards."

"I did nothing of the sort. And if she told you that, then she's lying." Jason picked up his notes before continuing. "What did she do, Sean, hunt you down and cry on your shoulder, hoping that I'd relent on my hold on her? Well, it won't work. She's my mate, and the sooner the little twit figures it out, the better off she'll be. I'm not going to coddle her, nor am I going to let her whine to my family about things she doesn't like or doesn't think I should do to her. She's my property and that's that."

"I think you should cool off." Dad was still standing between them, and looked like he wanted to hit Jason too. "I don't know what's going on around here, but I doubt very much she would have called any of us, thanks to you. But if you call her your property once more, I might finish what Sean started."

"There it is. It's all my fault. Did it ever occur to you what it was going to be like having a human female around all the time? That she'd be making demands on not just me, but all of us?" Sean told him he was full of shit. "Really? Because you're here right now pissed off at me because of something she said to you. Am I right?"

"No, you're wrong." Jason didn't want to believe him, but he knew that they could never lie to each other. "She didn't send me anywhere. I'm here because of how you treated her. How you act like you are so innocent in all this. Do you have any idea what she did to make this whole idea happen for herself? No, you don't. You're just blindly doing this because you're trying to make a point. Whatever it is, it's lost on her, and the rest of us. You should be ashamed of yourself."

"No. And would you like to know why? Because she had a fit and left me standing there after I spent my hard-earned money to buy this place." Dad pointed out that she'd told them not to buy it. "Yes, well, we all know that's what a woman says when she really wants to you purchase something for her."

"What happened to you?" He asked Sean what he meant. "To make you into this person who would think the worst of their mate? To go on and on about things you have no knowledge of, as well as no reason for it? What happened to make you into this bitter, horrific person that you are today? It can't be her, she's only been around for a few days. And in that time, you've crushed her dreams, hopes, and any kind of compassion she might have had for you. You truly are an asshat and a prick."

Jason moved away from them both. He wasn't at fault, and he wasn't going to stand there and take it. He heard Sean laugh and turned to look at him. But there was so much anger on his face that Jason found himself backing from him.

"She's lost it all. Her dad's insurance money. Her house too, as soon as they find out that she can't pay for the demands that the city is making on her. The little bit of food that she has in the house, very little, by the way, she offered to share with me." Jason didn't like that they were ganging up on him and told him that. "Don't worry, Jason, this will be the last time that I bring her up in any conversation that I have with you. Ever. I just wanted you to know that deep in her heart is a woman that, despite having nothing of her own, gives everywhere she can."

When Sean left him, he stood there with his dad. Dad didn't look any happier than Sean had, but Jason just ignored it for now. He was going to make this work and show them all that she'd only been in this for the cash.

"What do you need for me to do?" He asked him to not bring her up as well. "I was talking about this building. Like Sean, I don't want to talk to you about her either. What do you want done to his building?"

He was hard pressed not to just tell him to go the fuck away. It was his dad, after all. So, instead of saying what was in his head, Jason let out a long breath and told him of the plans that had been with the paperwork that Spencer had left him.

"I have a crew that can come in and clean the place up. That'll have to be done first and foremost. There is too much dust and rodents around for us to get a good bit of work going." He nodded and asked about the plumbing. "It's hooked up to the city, like we were told. And there is a special deal with the gas company that says for as long as the building is held by someone and not torn down, then that is free. Could be that we'd have to take them to court, but I've seen the paperwork and I think we can make it work."

They talked about the building for over two hours. Jason made notes on things his dad either suggested was needed and what needed to go. There was a lot of debris in the upper level. Also a great deal of office equipment, solid furniture that was made of hardwoods and brass. He decided to put it aside and see what they could get for it, to defray costs.

Heading to the offices that they had downtown, his dad was quiet, so much so that Jason could feel his temper flaring up again. But no matter how many times he asked if it was the woman, he'd not answer him. This shit had gone on long enough.

"I've decided that I'm going to find her and mark her. That way I can keep an eye on her while she's running around like she doesn't have a care in the world." Dad said nothing, not even a quirked brow at him. "She's out of hand if she's going behind my back and turning my family against me."

"If you think that then I'm afraid there is no hope for the two of you. If you don't need me anymore, son, I'm going to see what I can do about getting the crew to start on the building. The sooner we can get things going, the better it will be, I'm thinking." His dad headed to the door and turned back. Jason thought it was coming now, his dad telling him how disappointed he was in him. "There is one thing I was just thinking about. What if we try and salvage that roof? There is enough slate tile up there that we could sell it off to the right person for some nice cash."

"That's what you were going to say?" His dad nodded, looking confused. "You don't have a thing to say about Spencer and how I'm such a horrible person?"

"Nope. I told you, nothing from me."

Jason wanted to scream at him that this wasn't his fault, but his dad just walked away. Jason sat at his desk and tried to cool his head. Christ, this was a nightmare.

The phone ringing made him realize that he'd gotten nothing done in the two hours that he'd been home. Not only that, but he couldn't remember a single thing that he'd thought about other than that woman. He knew she had a name, but right now, he thought "that woman" suited her better. Answering the phone, he was surprised to hear from his banker.

"I have the deed to the building you purchased yesterday." He asked him what deed. "To the Spencer building you bought at the auction. The young lady brought it by this morning and asked me to make sure you got it. It's been notarized, by the way, and now has your name on it."

He wanted to hurl the phone across the room, then go and find that woman and beat her senseless. He had a feeling that he'd have to murder her before that happened. Calmly, as much as he could be under the circumstances, Jason told him to change it back.

"I can't do that, I'm afraid. If I do, then she'll sue. And she has a good case on her hands, so you know. You used your money to buy the place. You forged her name to the deed, and you had it notarized without her permission or consent. Jason, what were you thinking?" He told him it was her fault. "Spencer's? Well, I don't know about all that, but the deed is here whenever you can come to get it."

Hanging up the phone, he sat there again. Christ, the woman was driving him nuts. She was going to make it so that he'd have to take her under his wing to make sure that she didn't harm herself if she kept up with this craziness. Sitting there, he closed his eyes then snapped them open again.

"Good Christ." Jason had just realized something. He'd not fed before meeting her. And now, without her, he'd starve. She was doing this on purpose, he just knew it. Simply to hurt him, then take him for everything he had. "Damn it all the fuck and back. I suppose this was her plan to make sure that I fund whatever shit dream she has in her head. Mother fuck."

He got up and paced his office. She'd done this to back him into a corner. And the whole, "Don't buy it for me" kind of shit was planned too. He just knew it. That woman was going to kill him, and then more than likely dance on his ashes. Jason was so pissed off that he'd not realized that his vision had turned murky red and that his fangs had stretched from his mouth. Standing still, he calmed his inner beast and tried to get a handle on his anger.

"I'm going to have to go to her, figure out what she wants, and get her to let me live." He had no idea how to make her understand, and decided that he'd just have to fake it. Getting her to think he was romantic, when he was far from it, was going to have to work.

As he sat back at his computer, he realized he had no idea what she might like, or where she even lived. And he was sure that calling Sean would get him nowhere. He'd just have to figure it out on his own. He wasn't a stupid man, regardless of what the others said about him.

After two hours of calling in favors, he knew her address. He also had ordered two dozen red roses to be picked up by him, a car to be brought around so he'd not have to walk there, as well as dinner reservations at his favorite place. She'd better appreciate all the trouble he was going through for her. And the cost. Yes, he did have nearly limitless funds, but that didn't mean he was going to give her access to his money. Not one penny of it unless she was nice to him for a change.

It was late by the time he had things the way he wanted them. Much too late for him to go to her home. He decided to tell his dad where he was going, in the event that she murdered him, Dad would know who had done it. It wouldn't have surprised him in the least if his family was there helping her do the deed, and giving her all the information that she might need to make it work.

"They're all out of their minds. You'd think that a pretty girl wouldn't turn their heads like this. Like she's leading them around by their dicks." He stretched his neck, and felt better when it popped. He had too much to do to be hanging around a woman so that he could get on with his life. Jason felt that he wasn't being unreasonable, but he was pissed, and he thought that allowed him to be any way that he wanted. He was older than her, a man, and powerful. She should be thinking about how lucky she was that he was in her life. Christ, he hated this shit.

Staying up later than he had intended, he got as much work done as he could. There was still a lot to do, things that he couldn't take care of in the middle of the night, but he was quite pleased with what he'd been able to accomplish with the new project. Jason refused to think of it as hers; she'd had an idea, yes, but he'd yet to be duly appreciated for it. Going up to bed at around four in the morning, he was thinking of the list of things he'd left for Garrett to do. Mostly things like making the house ready for a female. She'd better not change anything either, was his last thought as he closed his eyes.

CHAPTER 4

"I'm sorry, Miss Graham, but for this job, we were hoping for someone on an entry level. You're overqualified. You'd be more suited to a supervisory position." She told the lady that was looking over her resume that she'd take that job then. "At this time, we're not in the market for a supervisor. I'm terribly sorry."

Leaving the store that had a help wanted sign on the door, Spencer wanted to scream. She was either too experienced or not enough. There had to be a job out there that she was a fit for. Where it was, however, was anyone's guess. The next place on her list was next to a bar. Deciding that she had time for a sandwich that she could ill afford, she went into the dark building and asked to be seated near a window.

Ordering a hamburger with no fries and a glass of water was much cheaper than she thought it should be. But she wasn't complaining. Cheap was cheap, and she had to be that way for the next few months. She pulled out the letter that she'd gotten that morning. The man that had brought it to her told her at least a dozen times that he was sorry. He said he'd been delivering them all day.

"You're gonna have a few weeks, miss, but not much more. The people that want this land, they're hoping to have everyone out in a couple of weeks. I think that we don't need any more cable lines here, nor do we have to take somebody's house to make them more money." She nodded. Spencer had been aware that she was going to lose her house soon. It was unfair, but she didn't have the means to fight city hall.

Reading it over, just to see if there was a loophole, she was surprised when someone sat across from her. Mr. Crosby smiled at her, but didn't say anything when he took one of the chips that came standard with her meal.

"You come here often?" She said she'd never been there before, and asked if he did. "No. When I was first here, I came by to.... Well, I used to come by at night after they closed."

"I see. I was hungry and decided that this place was as good as any." She picked up her burger after splitting it in half, and offered half to him. He said he'd only take it if she allowed him to get some fries, his treat. "Go ahead. I'm not going to be able to finish it all anyway. I've been feeling a little off."

"Nerves will do that to you." His fries were brought right out to them, and he had a glass of water too. Taking her portion of the burger, she munched on her chips while he ate the rest. "You find a job yet?"

"Do I even want to know how you found out that I was job hunting?" He just grinned at her. "I see where most of your sons get it from. You're about as charming as a ten-year-old little boy. As cute as one too. Don't you age at all?"

"Thank you. And not really. We can age ourselves, but once we hit a certain age, in this case about twenty-five to thirty, we don't age at all. As for being charming, I did used to charm women all the time. You know, it's easier for my kind to do that than to just take. I'd have to be very hungry just to bite a person for a meal. At least, I hope so." She nodded. "Do you have any questions for me? I can answer just about anything you want to know."

"No. Not unless you know someone that's hiring, or a place to live. I'm sure with your knowledge as to why I'm job hunting, you know it all." He said that he did. "How did you find out? Was it Sean? He said he wouldn't tell anyone."

"I didn't hear it from him. And if he told you he'd keep your secrets, then he will. We can't lie to you either. But about your home, I hang out at the courthouse sometimes. Just to remind myself that there are people out there that are worse off than I am. Usually, it's when I'm feeling sorry for myself. Anyway, today I went by to tell this buddy of mine that I'd not be around much. He's a sad sack, and I was feeling his pain too much and transferring it to my own cup of sorrow. I think all the negativity was making me too sad. Butch, he told me that a bunch of foreclosures were going out with him today. He had one with your name on it."

"They're not foreclosing so much as they're taking my house, because I can't afford to make the necessary improvements that are going down our street. Also, the cable company wants to put a large tower in my backyard and I wouldn't let them. Not so long as I own it. I guess they decided that if I wouldn't play ball, then they'd get someone working for them that would. I have ninety days to move or they'll tear the house down around me. But the cable lines and other improvements are saying I have three weeks, less if they can help me along by putting my things at the sidewalk." She put her half of the burger down, no longer that hungry. "Life pretty much sucks right now."

"I'm so sorry, honey." She nodded and drank her water

while she tried to control her hurt. "If it makes you feel any better, I can tell you that there are others trying to stop the cable company from taking over lands. The improvements, however, are still going to go through. Are you sure that you can't make arrangements with them?"

"I tried. I mean, at first they were going to allow me to get a loan that would do it. Then they decided that since I wasn't going to be able to pay up front, like the rest of the street was, they'd find other things that would kick me out on my ass. Mostly it was just small things, but it was enough for the courts to decide that my house wasn't livable. I lived there all my life, and because of progress, I can't anymore. Improvements aren't supposed to put you in the poor house or take your home from you, to my way of thinking." She decided to change the subject; there was no point in going over this again. "What are you doing around town today? I mean, it's really odd that you can be out like this, isn't it?"

"It is. We saved someone long ago, and she granted us the ability to be in sunlight." She told him that Jason had mentioned that. "Yes, it was the faerie queen. Her name is Kilian, and while she is magical, the attack on her home and her people hurt them badly. Had she died then all of mankind would have suffered greatly because of it. A lot of her kind were lost. We did try to save them all, but the fire was out of control and it was hot. Too hot for us."

"So, she gave you this gift and you've been living all this time. I'm not sure about living forever. I mean, I guess it would be good for some, but I don't have anyone that I hang around with, and I think I'd be bored really easily." She laughed when she thought of her life. "I'm thinking that being homeless and jobless would be a major problem when you have to live forever."

"It would be." She asked him about what he'd done in his many lifetimes. "I was a doctor for a while. I didn't care for it overly much. An attorney. That wasn't my cup of tea either. A racecar driver once. That was fun, but when I got hurt but didn't die in a horrific crash, people started asking questions. When you have the time, and the funds, which we do, you can pretty much do whatever you want. I've done about everything, from cook to make some shady deals too. But we all try our hand at things, just to see what glove fits us."

"I would imagine that you'd have to be careful of that. Walking away from something as horrific as an accident. People find out you can live forever and they start wanting to do tests on you and such." He nodded, and the waitress came and took their empty plates away. "I have to get going, I'm afraid. I need to find me some gainful employment, and soon."

"Can I help you?" Spencer told him she would be fine. "I know that Sean came to see you. He's got a soft heart. I used to think that was a bad thing, but the older he got, the more he took on projects that helped people get out of situations that were no fault of their own. And since the other day, I've been trying my best to do the same. It feels good, actually, to help others when you don't want to go on. I don't think that came out right."

"Yes, it did. I understood you. As for Sean, I like him. He's kind." Mr. Crosby laughed but didn't say anything. "And I like Grayson. He's scary smart, isn't he? I mean, when I was talking to him the other day at the auction house, he was spouting off information that was amazing. I guess that's because like you, they've done a few things that others wouldn't have gotten the chance at."

"Yes, he loved to read as a child. And never got out of the habit. I think that was his mom's doing. She so loved to read too." Standing up, she reached for the check when he did. "I have this. It isn't often that a man like me gets to take a pretty girl out to lunch. Next time, you can pay."

She had a feeling that when with this man, she'd never have to pay. Not that she'd be able to do this again, not unless she found herself a job, but it was nice to know that he wanted to spend time with her despite his son being a full out bastard. Spencer also had a feeling that Mr. Crosby knew she was broke. The money that she had for her lunch today was earmarked for gas money, and she'd have had to walk everywhere until the last of her profits from the purse sales came through.

Spencer left him in the parking lot while she went to the next store. By four that afternoon she was no closer to having a job than she had been when she left her house that morning. It was hot and she was hungry again, but also a little sick to her belly. She'd have to find some place to live, and soon. But without a job, she didn't know how she was going to swing deposits and what not. She fucking hated life right now.

Mr. Crosby was on the front porch when she walked up her sidewalk. Smiling, she told him she was glad to see him.

"I am you as well. I was wondering something. Do you play chess?" She told him she did as she unlocked the door. "You'll have to invite me in, love. Or we can play out here. The day is pretty enough for it. Whatever you want, I'm at your disposal."

She wondered how someone as sweet as him could have

raised such an asshole for a son. She knew that Mr. Crosby probably had a temper, but he'd never shown it in front of her. Spencer wondered if the boy's mother had been a nice person, and thought she'd have to be a saint to have been around six men all the time, and a charming flirt like her husband.

"Would you like to come in, Mr. Crosby?" He nodded and told her to drop the mister part, he was just Crosby. "First or last name?"

"Only one I ever went by until recently, when you needed both a first name and a last one. When the boys were younger, they were the sons of Crosby. Just that. You know, 'There goes Ryan, he's the son of Crosby.' I think it's why it worked out so well to just use it as a last name." Spencer told him about her name. "I wondered if you were somehow named after that building."

"Sort of, I guess. My mom, Jewel's, maiden name was Spencer. Her parents owned a great deal of land around here. My dad was working on the Spencer building, a big deal back then, when they met. She'd been there with her dad and boyfriend at the time. They took one look at each other and knew that they were meant to be together." Kicking off her shoes as she made her way to the kitchen, Spencer told him the rest. "Just before I was born, Mom was hurt at work. She fell against a desk or something, Dad was never clear about it, but she hit her head and it put her under a great deal of stress. Dad did tell me that she'd been having a hard time being pregnant. Mom nearly lost me a few times, and it took its toll on her and me. Anyway, they took me by C-section that afternoon, and she died before getting to hold me."

"I'm so sorry about that." She told him she'd been too young to miss her, but her dad had raised her well enough and encouraged her to be what she wanted. "If the Spencers had all that money and land, why didn't they help your dad out? Or is it a case of him not being good enough for their name?"

"That's exactly it. Mom married well beneath her and her station in life, according to her parents. They would have taken me, I guess, but Dad needed me. And I him. He told me years later that he should have let me go live with them. For a week after that, I cried myself to sleep, thinking that he didn't want me." Crosby told her that wasn't possible. "When you're eight years old, that is possible in your head. Anyway, they told Dad that if he had married someone like him rather than their daughter, then he wouldn't have missed me anyway, that people like him would have lots of kids by then. Dad, I think, was glad to break away from them. I know that I was."

She was having leftover roast, but he only wanted to play chess. Spencer was fine with that. The thought of leftovers wasn't anything she thought she could stomach right now. So, setting up her dad's old chess set, she poured them both a glass of tea and sat down with him. She had a feeling that he was the best thing she could have around her right now. A kind man.

~~~

Jason hated to oversleep. Here it was three in the afternoon and he was still at his house. He'd yet to pick up the flowers, and he was still trying to decide what to wear. Finally, in a fit of anger, he pulled the first thing he touched out of his closet and put it on, then drove to her house.

Jason wasn't feeling well. He knew that he should have fed days ago...his head was spinning, and when he'd cut himself shaving, he didn't even bleed. She would have to get off her high horse and let him have some of her blood, or he was going to tie her down and make her.

Ringing the doorbell, he waited for someone to come let him in. The sun was bothering him too, because he was so weak. It wouldn't kill him, but it was making it painfully clear that he wasn't feeding when he should have. As soon as she opened the door, he knew that he wasn't going to make it. And that, along with everything else he'd been through, made him pissy. Or in this case, more so.

"Here, I got you some flowers." Jason wasn't used to having to woo women. And he never dreamed he'd have to try this out on his own mate. "I'd like to be invited in."

The door slammed in his face and he just stood there. She was the most unreasonable person he'd ever encountered. Pounding on the door again, he shoved the flowers at her when she didn't say anything. He was pissed when they simply fell to the floor.

"What do you want?" It was on the tip of his tongue to tell her to behave, but he didn't get the chance. "If you think you can come in here and start spouting things off that you need or want, then you can stay out there. I have shit going on, and you aren't going to help."

He knew what she was going through. Hell, he knew it all. And if she'd just give him a minute to tell her that she was moving in with him, then she'd have less on her plate. Not that he cared if she wanted it or not, but she was going to come home with him today. Even if he had to put her into a deep sleep and take her there himself.

"Why are you being like this? Don't you know that I'm your mate and that I own you? Or do you care?" She said that she didn't. "Invite me in, Spencer, and we'll settle this once and for all. You've been childish long enough. And I for one have had enough of it. Let me in and I'll feed, then we can talk."

"No, I don't think so. You're not a nice person, and the thought of you being able to come and go in my home bothers me on levels that you can't believe. So, state your business, if you have any, and go away." He growled low in his throat. "That doesn't impress me either. Why are you here?"

"I have to feed, as I said. And since you're my mate, it must be from you. I don't like it any more than you do." She turned to her right and he saw his father there. In the house with Spencer. "Why is he allowed in and I'm not? Not to mention, he shouldn't be because I've not allowed it."

"Allowed it? What gives you any rights to allow anything in my life? He's here because, unlike you, he's a nice man." Jason looked at his dad when he laughed. "Is it true, Crosby? What will happen if he doesn't feed from me?"

"He'll turn rogue. Could be that he'll starve and die. And I know that you're tempted to just leave him out there, but he'd turn, die without feeding." She looked at him as his dad continued. "Of course, you don't have to invite him in after that...he'd have access to the house anyway."

"Dad, you're not helping me here. Since you're all cozy with her, tell her to invite me in before I have to resort to stalking her like an animal." His dad just looked at him. There wasn't going to be any help from him, so he looked at Spencer again. "You need to invite me in. You're being stupid, and I don't care for it. Plus, I'm growing weaker every minute."

He was getting weaker too. Jason hadn't meant to go this long, but life had gotten in the way. And this woman wasn't helping him. When he fell to the floor of the porch, he knew she was going to stand there and watch him perish.

"You can come in this one time, and no more." He wondered for a moment if Dad had told her that little clause, but was too grateful to care at the moment. "And no funny business. But now that I say that, I doubt very much you have a sense of humor. Unless you're watching a hanging or something. That probably gets your rocks off better than a comedian. So, what I mean is, no sex or touching, other than to get enough for you to survive. If you don't piss me off any more than you already have. Which, you should know, isn't hard for you to do."

He dragged himself into the front hall of her home and lay there. When she helped him by pulling his arms, Jason snapped at her, telling her not to drag him around like the dead. His head exploded in pain, then nothing.

When he woke, he was still on the floor and his dad was sitting over him in a chair. Jason tried to sit up and discovered that Dad had the chair legs over his body, holding him there. He asked him to move.

"No, not just yet. I wanted to tell you something first. And if you're in a position that makes it so you have to listen, then I'm going to use it. I've been thinking about what you guys told me the other day. About how I'm so negative." Jason asked him how long this was going to take. "Until I'm done. I bought me a recorder thing to tape myself when I talk. Just to keep on top of myself."

"Where is Spencer?" Dad told him she'd left. "Left? And you just let her? She has to help me out of this mess."

"No, I don't think she cares at the moment. You made her cry, in case you care." He didn't, not really. "Anyway, back to me trying to keep atop of myself. I would go home and listen to myself to see what I might need to do to improve my attitude. During my recording myself, I got a bit of you on it too. You are not a nice person, Jason. To anyone. Especially to that young woman. I think I knew that all along, but I never got it put right out there in front of me until I started to really listen to you. And see firsthand how out of control you've gotten. And you have, to the point where you're going to die a lonely and hungry man."

"Dad, in the event that you missed something, she's my mate. There are no rules about kindness." His dad pulled out the recorder and hit play instead of saying anything else. "What is this going to prove?"

"Listen." He did. For about ten minutes, when he realized that the horrific things being said were spilling from his own lips. Dad paused the recorder to explain the next conversation. "This was the other night when we were standing outside the auction house, and you were talking about her and how she was stupid. She's not, by the way."

He'd not only called her stupid, but several other names that weren't fit to be said. Not about someone's mate. Especially not his own. As he listened, he felt his heart hurt for the things he'd said and implied. When his dad paused it again, he told him to stop.

"No, I don't think so. This is from just today. When you got here. To be honest with you, I turned it on before coming in the room with you. I was going to catch you later and let you hear this, but when she knocked you on the head with that vase over there, I thought what the hell, now is as good a time as any. She hit you hard and broke one of the few things she has left." The recording was loud, or at least his voice was. He was demanding for her to do things. Not asking, not

68

being polite as he would normally have been.

Well, not lately, even before she came into his life, but he had once been considered a nice guy. He wasn't. Not even close to that. And his dad recording him, showing him just how right she'd been about him, brought it home. Hard and painfully.

As he listened he heard himself hit the floor after telling her to be fucking careful, and he knew this was when he became unconscious. Her reaction to it was to burst into tears. She cried bitterly before telling Dad to deal with him, that she was leaving. Long after it was shut off, he lay there thinking.

"What the hell is wrong with you, son? This, it isn't you. I mean it is, but I don't remember you being this hard on anyone like you are her. What caused you to turn this way?" He said he didn't know, only aware that at some point he'd become exactly what she said he was. A humorless prick. "She might be better off if you just let her be. You've already hurt her enough that I don't think you're going to be able to fix this. Damn it, boy, she's a good person, and you've turned her into a bitter woman in just three days of knowing her. And I like her, so do the rest of your brothers. You've shoved her away so much that it's doubtful that she'd let you feed even if you were about to expire."

"I don't know what to say." Dad told him he'd better think of something quick. "I don't even know where to begin. I've been.... Well, you know better than most what I've been. And none of this was her fault. She was just a person that I...I guess I thought I had to deal with."

"You sure made that clear enough, in that you didn't want to deal with her or whatever problems she might bring to you. Did it ever occur to you what sort of problems being your mate is going to be for her?" Jason told him that he hadn't. "That much is obvious. You don't deserve her. And if she leaves you to die, it won't be anyone's fault but your own. I may have driven you crazy wanting to join your mother, but at the rate you're going, you'll never know that sort of love. You got one chance at this, and you fucked it up, royally."

Dad stood up and pulled the chair off him. As he made his way to the door, Jason stayed where he was. He had one shot at this, one. Because if he left her home, he'd never be able to get back in. That much he knew better than most.

There would be no wooing this woman. He wasn't even sure if that was an option before he'd been such a horrible person. She wasn't one to fall at someone's feet just because they'd said something nice to her. Again, especially not after the way that he'd treated her. His dad might have gotten away with it, but not him, not any longer.

Flowers wouldn't work either. She didn't strike him as the type that would care for a vase of dying flowers. Unless, of course, they were something that might poison him. Jason thought that she'd be very willing to feed him something that would kill him. Sitting up, he looked around her house.

He knew nothing about her. Not one little tidbit that he could use. Getting up from the floor, he looked around at the things that she had, the pictures of her and her father. The small treasures he was sure that they had picked out together. Picking up a small snow globe of a zoo trip, he put it back where he'd found it and noticed that the house was spotless too. No dust marred any of the surfaces. There wasn't a cobweb in sight either. Going to her closet, he noticed that her things were hung neatly, all the hooks on the hangers going the same way. In her drawers were neatly folded under things. Not the sexy kind that he thought about her wearing, but serviceable things. Well-made and durable.

The larger pieces of furniture had tags on them. He thought that she'd just purchased them, and was trying to work them into his home. When he looked closer, he saw that they were for sale tags, that she was selling her things. Things he'd bet that she loved but needed the money more.

As he wandered around the little house, he saw parts of her that he was sure no one did. The empty refrigerator was probably the most depressing thing that he'd ever seen. He just stood there looking at it as he thought of all that she'd gone through, and he'd not any idea what it might have been. But he could see what it was costing her. Everything. And this, too, was his fault.

There was a quart of milk that had less than an inch in it. A covered dish that held a small bit of roast beef, a carrot, and parts of a potato. Packets of butter, a container of tea, and another one of juice. Going to the cabinets after closing the door, he found them just as bare as the pantry. There was a single plate in the cabinet with a cup. And in the sink, there was one that didn't match either of the other pieces, a glass from some restaurant, as well as a mug that was shaped like a canning jar. Things, he'd bet, that she'd picked up at a sale or something.

Jason sat down at her table and realized that she was on the edge of poverty. Then he remembered what Sean had told him. She had banked on the building that he had lorded over her. And when he'd done that, he'd taken more than just her pride and her way to make a living, he'd hurt her too. Jason wasn't proud of himself.

He wasn't sure what to do now. He had to do something

to make up for what he'd done, what he'd taken from her because of his behavior. This was beyond him starving and needing to feed from her. This was his mate, and he had to make it up to her for how he'd been treating her.

"Christ, I've been such a fool." If she were here, he had a feeling that she'd agree with him. He had to do something, but first he needed information. And he was going to have to do some major sucking up to get it from the two people that he knew had it. Dad and Sean.

CHAPTER 5

It was dark when she made her way back home. Spencer hoped that Jason had grown tired of waiting and left. Of course, with him, he'd more than likely just stay there and she'd have to deal with him. Even going to talk to her dad at his grave didn't help her with any answers.

She visited him when she could. Most weeks she'd go at least once, but lately it was a couple of times a week. Spencer told him what had happened, how she'd banked on a man that didn't want her to, nor did he think she'd succeed. Then she told him about being his mate.

"He's worse than I ever thought a man could be. Just like grandfather, I'm assuming. I wish you would have told me about him, Dad. I don't know what I might have done, but I could have helped us a little." She picked up the paper marker that had been laminated so many years ago it was faded with time. "The next time I come, I'll bring you a better one. Maybe a few pictures of the bags I'm making too."

The lights were on in her house when she went up the walkway, but that might only mean that she'd not turned them off this morning. But it was the smells coming from the kitchen when she entered that had her pausing. She either had a strange burglar or Jason was still there. When he came out of the kitchen, she turned her back to him.

"Please, don't leave again. I'd like to tell you I'm sorry." She didn't speak. Her question to him might have been "For which thing are you sorry?", but there were just too many to list. "I made us dinner and thought that, if you're willing, we can enjoy a nice meal and then talk. I promise you, just talk."

"You mean demand and scream at me. Or is it to call me a fucking moron again, or stupid? All names that you've called me over the past few days." He nodded and said again he was sorry. "I don't believe you."

"No, I wouldn't imagine that you would. And for that, I'm profoundly sorry." She said nothing to him. "Come into the kitchen and we'll eat. I didn't know when you'd be back, so all I have to do is cook the steaks."

"I don't have steaks. Even if I had any, I'd not have enough to share with anyone. I'm on a tight budget." But he was gone, and to find out where the steaks had come from, she followed. "What have you done?"

Her table was set with new plates, and not the chipped and broken ones she'd been using. There was a candle in the middle of it all, with a dozen or so roses in a vase. She could smell them, even from across the room. The plates had foil wrapped potatoes, green beans, and still steaming bread. The crock of what appeared to be butter wasn't hers, but she liked the nice little touch. She looked at Jason when he said her name.

"This is nice, but I can only think that you've bullied someone into bringing you what you needed and you're going to blame this on me. If you don't mind, I'd like for you to say whatever it is you need to and get out. I don't have the heart to listen to you berate me again." He nodded. "Why did you do this?"

"My family brought me what I needed. After much groveling. Dad brought the roses. He said to make sure you knew they were from him for the good games of chess." She asked him why he'd bothered. "Because I needed to tell you I'm sorry."

"You're hungry, that's all. I talked to a friend of mine. He said that you weren't lying to me about that part." He nodded and asked her to have a seat. "I don't know about this, Jason. You're not a nice person, and once I start to eat — I'm hungry too — I don't want you to spoil it all by being yourself."

"If you'll sit with me and have dinner, I promise to be on my best behavior." She asked him if he remembered how to do that. "It's been a long time, I'll admit that, but I think I can remember it. I'm not...I wasn't always like I have been lately. And it's not you. I was being a bastard to everyone I was around."

"Your dad told me." She sat and was astonished when he helped her sit closer to the table. "He said that you used to be so calm and forgiving. I think I might have liked that version of you."

Jason sat down. It was then that she noticed how pale he was, how his fangs were stretched from his upper teeth. She wasn't as afraid as she might have been before talking to her friend, but she was nervous. He jumped up again and said he'd forgotten the steaks.

"I rarely cook anymore. When we were first changed by the queen, we did it a lot, just to try new things. For me it was a treat to be able to find out about sweets. Not that I could gain any weight from overeating, but I did try hard. I was eating bags of chocolate, the dark rich kind, for every meal. I think I burned myself out on it." While he babbled, because she was sure that was what he was doing, Spencer fixed her potato. There was sour cream, the good kind that didn't have a layer of water over it that had to be mixed in. Bacon slices that smelled like heaven, and chives that had been cut up in small pieces and were fresh, she could tell. Butter too, which she slathered all over not only her potato, but her roll as well. "Well, what do you think?"

"I'm sorry. I was...I was paying more attention to my meal than you. I've not.... I'm sorry." He grinned and told her that was fine. "I can't remember the last time I had a steak, much less someone to wait on me. I can afford a burger now and then, but not much lately. And the condiments that you've gotten are a real treat for me. Like I'm having a fancy meal in a big restaurant. You must think I'm a dork."

"No, I don't. And all of this, it's my fault." She asked him how that was even possible. "I don't mean entirely my fault, but I do know that you sank a lot of your own money into this project, and I fucked that up for you."

"You did." She wasn't sure that she could eat now, her belly wasn't happy.

"Spencer, you should know that the building is being renovated to your specs. There is a crew going over it from top to bottom right now to make sure that it's sound. I think it is, but they want to make sure. You have a good head on your shoulders, but I'm sure you know that."

"I like to make things." She picked up her fork and steak knife, only planning to take a bite of her dinner now. "Once when I was younger, I had it in my head that there needed to be a way to travel with a hook on your pole without it getting all hooked up in everything around it. I used what we had around the house to figure it out, and finally came up with using a toilet paper sleeve with a rubber band around it. It worked, but not well enough. I think it took me a couple of months to get it so that it worked."

"I think that's brilliant. I've never been fishing myself. I don't know why, but it wasn't anything my dad did, so we probably didn't think of it either." She took a bite of her steak and moaned. "Christ."

Looking at Jason, she wondered for a moment what she'd done. The look on his face, the way his body was stiff, had her standing up and going to him. Putting her hands on his shoulders, she was surprised when he stood and backed from her, and she could see that he was in a great deal of pain.

"What is it?" He growled and her body reacted. Not in fear, but need. "You're.... There is something wrong with you, I think."

"Yes." His voice was slurred, his eyes were dark with blood. "Back away from me, please. I don't want to harm you. Nor to take what you don't want me to have."

"Blood." He nodded, then shook his head. "Sex too? Is that why you did all this? To make me all soft and gooey for you?"

"You moaned." It took her mind a moment to figure out what he was talking about. "I have to leave here now. I don't want to. You won't allow me access again, but you aren't safe around me."

"You'd hurt me?" He nodded, and then again, shook his head. "This is getting me nowhere. What the fuck are you talking about?"

"I'm hungry. You're my mate. If I take from you, it won't be the only thing I want. Not just your blood, but all of you. I cannot feed from anyone else." She nodded and he growled. "Don't you see? I want you, all of you. And I won't take it simply because you think I tricked you into it. A few hours ago I would have, if it would have gotten me what I wanted. But I'm not going to do that, not to you. I want to be a better man. I can be a better man."

She found herself alone in the kitchen. Not only had he left her, but he'd also failed to let her answer him. Yes, she might have thought that he had tricked her, but there wasn't any reason for him to take off right in the middle of a conversation. Just as she sat down, Sean appeared in the room. Smiling, he sat down.

"Jason sent me." She asked him why. "Because, and this is his words, not mine, he'd 'fucked up enough with you, he wasn't going to start anything that might have you trust him less.' He's not doing well."

"As in he's going to turn because of his hunger." Sean nodded, then like his brother, shook his head. Spencer had enough and slapped him. "Answer me right. This nodding and shaking the head is stupid. Tell me. All of it. Or I swear, the next time I'm with one of you, I'm going to feed you garlic and then stake you."

"You're a spitfire, aren't you? He is hungry, but that's not all of it. He needs his mate. Your body and your blood. Now that he's found you, his inner beast, the vampire in him, has surfaced, and he could harm you. Would more than likely kill you in the state that he's in." She asked him about the law or whatever that forbade him hurting her. "He won't know that he is…his beast is hungry like he is."

"I don't understand. He can have food. Why isn't that appeasing his beast?" She watched his face and got it when

78

he flushed. "Sex. It's not just food, but sex too. I thought that was a myth."

"There are a lot of myths out there, but that one is true. The two of them, the beast and Jason, need you to come to them willingly. Jason knows that he's screwed up, but—" He stood up and looked out her window. "I have to go."

Spencer grabbed him before he could. "What happened? Where is he? Tell me, or so help me, I will kick your ass."

"Do you want to be his mate?" She nodded, not even sure why she was saying yes. "Are you sure? There will never be any turning back, Spencer. The two of you will be mated forever. You'll never be alone either. You have a large family now that loves you."

"Yes. Take me to him."

Before she could tell him that she was going to get something else to wear, she was standing in the woods alone. She looked around when she heard something howl. It wasn't until it was nearly on top of her that she realized it was Jason.

~~~

The little part of Jason that he could hold onto told his beast to not hurt her. That she was their mate for all time. But he snarled at him that she was his, and Jason tried to pull from the monster inside of him. Spencer stood very still, and he was glad for that. If she ran, it would be over.

"Spencer? Don't move." She nodded at his dad and his beast swiped at him. "Behave, you shit. I'm here to protect her from you. What the hell do you think you're doing but scaring the life out of her? Haven't you been bad enough as her mate? Now settle down and let me help you both."

Dad would understand what he was feeling more than anyone would. As he made his way to Spencer, he talked calmly to her, telling her why he was there.

"Sean said that you'd need someone to tell you what he wants, and why. I think you understand the why of it or you'd not be here." Spencer said that she understood. "Good, honey. All right. The beast, his monster, wants to hurt you for taking so long to come to them. You just have to be...Well, honey, you have to be yourself and put him in his place. Don't let him bully you or hurt you. All right? If he knows that you're not going to take his shit, then he'll behave himself. He'd better anyway."

"You mean I'm to smack him around." Dad laughed and said that was the ticket. "I don't know...have you seen him? He only looks like Jason because that's the shirt he had on when he left me there."

Jason knew what he looked like. His fangs were long, about an inch out of his mouth. His eyes were blood red from the anger, and his body was bigger, much larger than he'd been as a man. Looking at his hands and feet, he saw that his claws had come out, and his shoes were no longer on his feet. He was, just as his dad had said, a monster.

"You can do it. I'm sure of it." The monster in him moved closer, not listening to him as he told him to back off. "Don't run, Spencer. If you do, then he will most assuredly hurt you. Just let him take his time sniffing at you."

"All right. But if he does anything that I don't think he should, then I'm going to knock the shit out of him." The beast growled and Jason laughed. She was doing this willingly, yes. But he could also tell that she was terrified out of her mind. Spencer got down on her knees and looked at him. "I'm not going to take your shit, buddy. I've had a shitty day and you're just about to fuck it up for me. And for the first time in longer than I care to remember, I was going to have a nice steak and a lovely baked potato, and you fucked that up as well. What the hell, Jason? Will anything ever be just normal with you?"

He knocked her to the ground and sniffed her neck. When she kneed him in the groin, Jason's monster jumped off her and snapped his teeth at her face. Spencer smacked him upside the head, hard enough that he was sort of crossed-eyed when he looked at her.

"Stop that shit right fucking now. This isn't the way things are done, and I'm sure you know it. Do you want me to be afraid of you all the time?" The monster whimpered. "Now, we're going to go at this slowly, or so help me, I'll make what you're feeling right now seem like a day in the park. Sit."

He sat down on his ass and Jason could feel his confusion. Glancing at his dad, he knew that he was enjoying this a little too much. Dad was holding onto the tree while laughing like a fool. So long as he hung around until he could control himself around her, he was fine with him laughing.

"Are you listening to me?" He nodded. "Good. How do we make it so we can have a conversation? I'd like to talk to him, but I don't want him to embarrass himself in front of you, Crosby."

"He needs a wee bit of your blood. Don't let him bite you. He might take that as a good sign. Just...Can you cut yourself a little bit and let him lick it?"

"Do you have a knife?" He tossed her one and Spencer picked it up. Before she cut herself, she looked at him again. "You lunge at me, knock me down again, and I'll cut my wrist and die while you watch. Understand?"

The beast nodded. When the scent of fresh blood hit his

nostrils, he felt him stiffen. Jason could see that it was indeed a small cut, but he didn't care. Food. That was all his beast wanted, but never moved toward her.

"You can come here and taste this, but you take anymore and that'll be it for you. Understand?" He nodded and moved toward her, careful not to go too fast. "You've been a terrible person, by the way. Scaring your family like this. I feel like I've asked this a million times of you, but what the fuck is wrong with you? You don't strike me as stupid. Mean and full of shit, but not stupid."

The beast licked her hand and sealed the wound. Then he did the same to her face. As he sat down again, Jason felt more in control of himself. Like he could be the one in charge rather than the monster. When he took a little of himself back, he stayed still.

"You're here." He said that he was. Jason decided that there'd be no more nodding to her. It was painful. "You scared me. Don't do that again."

"I'm sorry." She nodded and looked toward where his dad had been. He was leaving them now, and Jason wondered if he thought they'd be all right. He certainly didn't. "I'm a fool."

"You're not going to get me to disagree with you. What were you thinking, being in the same house with me like you were?" He told her he thought he was bigger than it was. "Yes, well, that didn't work out so well, now did it? You tasted my blood. Was that all it took to feed you so that you'd be all right?"

"No." He wasn't going to lie to her, not that he thought he could, but this was something that scared even him. "I might turn back again, but for now, I have some control over him. I'm very sorry that I frightened you and the rest of my family."

"You need what from me now?" He didn't know how to answer her. Jason knew that she didn't trust him, and he couldn't blame her. "You need me, now. Don't you?"

"Yes. Very much so. I've gone too long. I know that I might hurt you." She said she understood that. "You said you were having a shitty day. What happened that upset you?"

"Are you going to fly off the handle again?" He promised her that he'd try not to. "I guess that's good enough. I received my eviction notice a couple of days ago. I can't find a job that will pay enough in the short time I have to pay a deposit as well as the first month's rent. I will get some money from the sale of my house because it's paid off, but it'll come too late for me."

"I have a house." She glared at him. "I mean, I have a house that is large enough for the two of us to live in without ever talking to each other. I hope that we will, but it's big even by my standards. If you would, I'd like for you to come and stay with me as we work this out."

"You have high standards, do you?" He smiled. "I thought so. Look, I don't even know if you might like to have sex with me again, if we do it. You might think I'm boring—"

Jason shoved her to her back and covered her with his body. Christ, she fit him. Groin to pelvis, breast to chest. Licking along her throat had her warming, her body ready for him. Lifting his head, he looked at her and saw desire there, need too. Her tongue moving over her lips, making them moist, had him rocking into her.

"Do you really think that I'd not want you more than just once?" She said others hadn't. "They're fools. I want you now and forever. I want to slide into you, feel you quake with your release. Relish in your body tightening around mine as you scream out my name."

"Jason, I'm not any good at—"

He kissed her. Jason had wanted to go gently, take her mouth softly, but when she moaned, he felt his beast snarl at him again and gave him what he wanted. And they both wanted their mate.

Her clothing was in shreds, his shirt was pulled off him. Jason wasn't sure who was doing the most damage to their clothing, but her warm body was beneath his, his cock straining to enter her. Taking her mouth again, he lifted her up to him, her ass cupped in his palm. And when he felt her body wrap around him, Jason slammed forward, filling her like he'd never experienced before.

"Yes." Her scream of release startled him. "Please. More, I need more. Jason, please, take me."

Jason took her...there was no foreplay, not this time. Their need was too high. When she offered her neck to him, he didn't think to ask, to see if she was all right with it, but sank his teeth deeply into her throat. She was his, she was submitting. That was what they both needed for now.

The blood filled his mouth, every pore of his body, until he was dizzy with it. As she screamed out his name over and over, Jason bit open his wrist and put it over her mouth. Sealing the wound at her throat, he watched as she drank from him. The first swallow, he felt it as if she'd caressed him. That was all it took to send him over the edge.

It was as if he'd been turned inside out. His body ached he'd come so hard. Every part of him was giving her everything. And when she screamed that she was coming too,

Jason bit her again as he emptied himself deep within her.

He knew as soon as he opened his eyes that he'd fainted. Looking down at Spencer, he could see where he'd been too rough on her. Her throat was bruised, her lips bloody. Licking the wound so that it would close, he saw her look at him with one eye, and smiled as she fell back to sleep. Jason thought he could go his entire life now on just that one simple gesture.

Rolling off her, he sat up. They were both naked, and it looked as if they might be heading back to the house that way. As he sat there in the quiet woods, he thought of all the things he was going to do for her. Starting with her dad's marker.

He had seen it in her mind when he'd first taken her blood. Or at least his beast had. She had wanted something small, just with his name and dates on it. It would sit next to the one that was for her mom. But that wasn't the only thing that he'd seen. For one so young, she had gone through some terrible, sometimes horrific, things in her life. He looked at her when she stirred a bit.

"You okay?" She told him she was fine, but when she moved he could see that she was in pain. "I might have been a little rough on you. I'm so sorry. But good gracious, woman. You turned me out and over just now."

"Thanks, but could you please stop saying you're sorry for a little bit? You've said it a dozen or so times since this evening." She looked around. "It's late, isn't it?"

"Yes, nearly midnight. Would you like to see something?" She stretched and he felt his cock do the same. "Come here, sit on my lap. But you should be very quiet. They only come out at night."

He wasn't sure she was going to since they were both naked. But he hurried her along when he started to see movement. As soon as she sat down, he put his hand over her mouth and pointed to the trees in front of them. He knew the exact moment she saw them.

CHAPTER 6

Spencer wasn't sure this wasn't another one of his tricks when he put his hand over her mouth and told her to be still. She wanted to smack him, but she saw movement and stilled. When something pulled from the tree in front of them, all she could do was stare.

She's a wood nymph. I don't see them often in the city, but they're on my — I mean our — lands a great deal. It's a safe zone for them, I guess you could call it. And when they come out, I try to be close enough to see them. They're very calming. The creature moved over the tree then down to the ground. Spencer watched as she touched the grass in front of her, then touched the tree. *She's making sure that the trees are doing well.*

The woman was about a foot and a half tall. She was what Spencer guessed was clothed, but it looked like bark from the tree. Her hair was green like the leaves that she was touching now, and her eyes were as dark as the night. Spencer knew that the only reason she was seeing her was because the moon was in a position that shone on her.

As they watched, she checked on several of the trees and even the grass around them. Then a small little man, no bigger than a lightning bug, came to fly in front of her. She pointed at them, then went back to her business. The little man came to them and sat on her leg.

"You're beautiful, my lady. I'm glad to see you've found someone." She nodded. "Here, let me help you."

Her body was clothed then, as was Jason's. The little man bowed when she thanked him quietly, and he moved to her shoulder. She could hear him well, but when he began talking to her from his new position, Spencer felt as if she was being given something no one else had ever heard before, nor had ever seen.

"Her name is Fairaday. She is the princess of these woodlands. Her job is harder than most because of the houses around here, but she keeps the trees in top shape, and has been for a great many years." Spencer asked him what he was. "Well, my lady, I am a nymph as well, but I am not a worker. I'm only a watcher. My job is to keep her safe. My name is Spud."

"Spud, thank you for this. What can you tell us about this forest and the Princess Fairaday?" Spencer looked at Jason, and he smiled at her as he continued. "This is my mate. She's new to this kind of discovery."

"Oh well then, I can tell you plenty. The trees here about get a fair amount of sun and water, but it's not always the best of liquid. There is trash about, as you can see, that hurts the trees when it tangles in the branches. Fairaday does her best to keep them free of the branches, but it is hard with so much of it about." Spencer watched Fairaday pick small bits of plastic out of the tree and stood up to help her. "Miss?"

She might have thought it a warning, for her not to tread too closely, but she could help and she wanted to. Reaching above the nymph's head, she pulled down a large piece of paper, as well as some string that looked like it was from a kite. Spencer asked the woman what she wanted her to do with them.

"I use them for nests. Or if I can find one, put them in the receptacles near the homes. You keep yours behind your home, which I use often. When you do not lock them. I cannot unlock the heavy locks." Spencer told her that she'd buy one for her to use and make sure that it had none. "Thank you, my lady."

They worked for several hours. When the sun started to crest, Fairaday told her that she must go. Spencer didn't want the magic to leave her, the magic of friendship. She'd found a friend in the woman even though they'd not spoken but the one time about trash.

"I should like to help you. All the time. Besides the trash can, is there something else I can do?" She looked to her right, and she knew that either Jason or Spud had come to join them. "I will not forget this night. You've given me a gift like none other. And I enjoyed helping you."

"Salt." Spencer asked her what sort. "I don't know the word. I hear so much, it is why I can speak to you so well, but it is like a box. If you could put it out for the other animals, I can have their droppings for the other plants."

"Manure. And it's simply called a salt block." Spencer smiled. "I can do that. I can also find you other things should you want. Tell me, and if I can do it, it'll be yours."

They both looked at Jason and Spud. The little man looked like he had a request, but was afraid to say anything. When she put out her hand, Spencer was surprised and delighted when he landed in her palm and smiled up at her. She asked him what he wanted.

"A bit of water wouldn't be remiss. And a few flower

petals if you can get them. We eat them." She nodded, then thought of something. "If you'd be so kind, that is."

"Yes of course. But the house, it's being torn down. I don't know when, but I have to move soon. And I don't know where I'm going yet." Jason put his arm around her and she leaned back on him. She supposed it was because of what they had just shared or something, but that didn't mean that she trusted him fully. Not yet, at any rate. "I don't own this land back here, but I bet that they'll get into your woods too. I'm so sorry."

"They'll tear down your house? Whatever for?" She told him about the sewage lines and the cable company, but only the highlights. "I'm sorry for that. I am. What will you do?"

"I don't know." Jason cleared his throat and she looked up at him. "I'm not sure about a lot of things at the moment. I'm sort of...I'm overwhelmed, if you want to know the truth."

Jason nodded and spoke. "I can understand that. We'll figure out something. In the meantime, I was wondering if you'd consent to coming to my house for the day. To get to know each other." She wasn't sure, and looked at Fairaday. "I live outside of town, not far from here."

"You'll be safe here, won't you? I mean, until I can figure out what to do for you? I don't know if we can save your trees, but I think we can find you a place to live. All right?"

"My lady, you would do this for me?" Spencer nodded and told her she would. "You are all kindness. We have never met a human like you before. Yes, I will be safe here. And should you not find a place, you aren't to worry. The queen, Kilian, will find a place for me. Much destruction goes on all the time. I hate to leave, but I know that sometimes it is necessary. And you giving me this warning means that I can get the other creatures out safely as well. There are a great many of us living here."

When they left the little area, she felt tears fill her eyes. Her first friend, and she was going to have to lose her to another field. Jason helped her clean up their uneaten dinner and wash the dishes, but her mind was on the nymph and Spud. Before she could guess his intent, they were in his car headed to breakfast.

"I'm not sure that I can eat." He told her that was all right, but she needed to drink juice. Because of what he'd taken from her. "Oh, yes, I guess so."

"Spencer, we can just go to our house and have breakfast if you don't want to go out." She looked at him. "It's no problem. They'll feed you over me anyway. I've been taking a lot of my shitty mood out on them too. Lately, everyone is telling me what a prick I am."

"You're just a whole lot of pain in the ass, aren't you?" He laughed, and she had to turn away from him. It was the sexiest thing she'd ever heard in all her short life. "Yes, at your house would be better. And I'm not so sure about meeting them today, but if they've put up with you and your moods, then I should be fine. I'm not...I've had a really rough few days."

She'd been to his house before, of course. But she'd been pissed then and hadn't paid any attention to the house or the occupants.

When they pulled up in front of the mammoth house, she could only stare. Good heavens, it looked like a hotel. She certainly didn't remember that. When he opened the car door for her, she almost told him to take her home. This wasn't a house for the faint of heart.

The front hall was something out of a fairy tale...long

staircase, big vases that more than likely cost more than her house, and silken wallpaper, with plenty of pictures that looked to be original works of art hanging from long chains. There were rugs too, beautifully done, the colors faded just a little from the sun gleaming in through the windows. Now she was here to enjoy the day, and she wasn't sure this was a good idea. She might not want to leave.

"No one will hurt you." She asked him if she would have a guide with her all the time. "You get used to it. It's big, yes, but laid out well. Come on, they'll think you don't want to meet them."

"I'm not sure I do. They'll expect someone that knows what they're doing." He asked her what she meant. "You know, how to be a person that lives in this sort of house. I don't know if I can pull it off."

Jason got down on his knees and took her hand in his. He looked so sad that she told him she was sorry. He kissed her hand then put it to his cheek. She knew he was going to tell her that it was all a joke, that he really wasn't her mate and that she was going to be shit out of luck. For what, she wasn't sure, but she knew she was going to be alone again.

"I don't know what you think you need to know about living in this house, but I'm sure that no one here will care if you came from the dumpster, so long as they have the pleasure of serving you. And for them, it will be a pleasure." She asked him why. "Because they're old, like I am, and have been only serving me for more years than you can imagine. They are sick of dusting a house that no one comes to. Polishing silver that no one uses, and cooking only for themselves. Trust me when I tell you, they're going to be as excited and nervous as you are to have you living here."

"I never said I'd live here." He grinned and stood up, putting out his hand again. "I never said I was going to live with you, Jason. I'm only here for breakfast. Just breakfast."

He was still laughing when they entered the room to the left of the great hall. The big man, Garrett, welcomed her home. Spencer thought she might be in trouble here.

~~~

"Did you see this?" Lloyd Spencer handed the paper to his wife. "Is this about that Graham person that married our daughter and killed her? What was his name? Yes, Chad. Such a common name too."

"How would I know? It says here that this person's first name is Spencer. Oh, I see, Graham. I don't know. How would we find out? Not that we should care, do you think?" He told her to read who the chit was marrying. "Crosby. Crosby. Why does that name sound so familiar?"

"That's the family, the Crosby family that has all the money in the world. Per the Journal. What on earth is that man thinking, marrying a half breed of a person, when he could have anyone he wanted? She'll never be the sort of woman that he needs at his side. Why, she's half blue collar, and that will never do." Lloyd pulled out his cell phone and called his attorney. For as much as he was paying him, he'd better answer on a Sunday. "Wendel. I have an issue I'd like for you to look into for me. There's an announcement in the paper for a Spencer Graham marrying someone by the name of Crosby. Can you find out who they are and who they're related to? I think I might know, but I want to be sure about it. There are all sorts of upstarts around the world just wanting to make a buck off a name."

"Yes, sir. I can do that. But you should know that Jason

Crosby is one of the Crosbys that owns a great deal of property here and there. It is rumored that his family has had money for more generations than people can track." Lloyd told him to find out who the girl was then. "I'll have you something today if I can find it."

Lloyd closed his phone and took the paper back. He read over the article, announcing the engagement of Crosby to someone named Graham, three times before he put the paper on his lap. There wasn't any way that this man, a smart one by all accounts, would marry so far beneath him. And if this thing was related to the murderer of his daughter, then he was going to have to step in and make him see reason.

"Sir, there is a phone call for you." Lloyd asked who it was; he did not do regular business on the weekend unless it was an emergency. And even then, he would have to put the person in their place. "It's Mr. Wendel, sir. He would like for you to be near your computer, he told me."

"Fine." He made his way to the office and turned the computer screen on as he picked up the phone. "You found something already? That was quick, even for you."

"You're not going to believe this. And you really don't need your computer. I just didn't know what you wanted your wife to know. It's your granddaughter." Lloyd just knew it. The man was going to be a part of his family via a granddaughter that he didn't want anything to do with. He asked him if he was sure. "Yes. I had no trouble getting information because she's in the middle of a big deal with the city. Bought a building and is opening a manufacturing company that will employee a lot of people. The man I have at the paper said that when all is said and done, they'll be in the black after only being open for six months, the way they have it figured. It's the old Spencer Building that you sold off a few years back."

"How can this be? She doesn't have.... Oh, I see. So, she's gotten herself in good with the money man, convinced him to marry her for some reason, and now she's going to be opening her own little business. What is she making? Rugs from a loom? Flowers from used toilet tissue or something like that?" He told him. "Gift bags? What the hell is so special about gift bags? Christ, she's as stupid as her father, and no better. I guess the apple doesn't fall far from the tree. Both of them, money grubbing idiots that will drain someone dry before they're finished. Set me up with an interview with this Crosby person. I'm going to save him a lot of heartache like I wished someone had for me."

He sat there for several minutes after hanging up, and decided to find out what he could about Crosby. There was a great deal to be had, if you had contacts in high places. Which Lloyd had cultivated quite nicely over the years. As he filled in the information that was needed to do his search, he thought of his daughter.

Jewel had been everything her name had implied. She was the apple of his eye and the reason his heart beat when she was a child. He'd take her to work with him, just to have her nearby in case he wanted to have some laughter. She was forever getting into things that would have made any other parent upset, but not him. Lloyd was so happy to have her that he knew that he had indulged her too much.

As she got older, however, he noticed that she had a mind of her own. A will to match it too. Terrible temper when she didn't get her way, so he found himself going to extreme measures with her. And no matter how many times he'd tried to bring her to heel, to make her see things his way, she would venture away and make decisions that he thought were wrong. Like marrying Graham.

Lloyd had forbidden it. Not even to date the low life. The man, he tried to tell her, only wanted one thing, and that was her money. Lloyd had even locked her in her room to keep her safe.

There were times when he still could not believe that she'd gone ahead and married the man. He'd forbidden her to do so, and she'd gotten around him by going to the courthouse and having one of those quickie weddings. And they'd been married an entire month before he'd gotten wind of it, and they'd not let him have it annulled. So, Lloyd did the next best thing and had them both cut out of his life. Lloyd just realized something. He'd have to take care of his will. He'd not done that, and now that this chit had resurfaced, he didn't want any more to do with her than he had her father. Especially when it came to his money. Lloyd did not like to be thwarted.

He was still sitting there looking up things about the Crosby family when his wife joined him. She was complaining about how he'd abandoned her and Lloyd ignored her. There was only so much whining that he could take. His wife, of late, seemed to be making it her life's work to drive him nuts with it.

"Lloyd, what is it you think you're going to do? Why does it matter to you who this young man marries?" It was a valid question, but he didn't care. "Lloyd, I'm speaking to you."

"I hear you. I have been hurt by Jewel's asinine decisions for a long time. And I'd hate to see someone else suffer the way that I have." That wasn't it, not really. But he'd not been able to make Graham suffer—he never rose to the bait—but he would his granddaughter. "You know as well as I that we could have done a better job of raising that brat of Jewel's. He was always one step ahead of us when we went to get her. I don't understand how a man that stupid could have slipped by us so much."

"Yes, and when we did finally catch up with him, the girl was no longer trainable. I'm very happy that we left her with him. But now? I'm not so sure. What if she comes after us for money? Or worst yet, she lets someone know who we are to her and that we never helped them?" He asked her who would believe someone like her. "But you said the Crosbys have money. Perhaps they'll want to know."

"The very reason that I'm going to have a word with the man as soon as possible. I'm going to set him right on a few things. Such as, how low he is marrying beneath him. Which reminded me, we have to take care that the chit won't get a thing out of us. I'll set up a meeting with Wendel this week sometime. I don't know why we didn't do it before now." A man like Crosby would want to know these things. Even if he was old money, he should know that this sort of behavior was frowned upon in their circles. "I'll have a talk with him, and then I'll consent to him using our attorney, who is used to this sort of work, to get rid of her right away. Before it's too late."

Lloyd started a list of things the man should be aware of. How Chad Graham had worked for him as a carpenter, of all things. That he'd stolen away his daughter in the middle of the night.

Well, that wasn't quite true either. She'd left the house one afternoon to meet her mother for lunch, and never returned. It was days later that he found that she'd emptied both her checking and savings accounts and sold her car to be with the beggar. He hated that she'd been able to pull something over his eyes. Lloyd supposed that was why he'd hated Graham so much. He'd gone and lowered his daughter to his standards.

"Perhaps it would be best if we said we didn't know about the child. That way, no one but us will know why we didn't have anything to do with her." He liked that idea, but didn't want his wife to think she had done something before him.

"I have it here already. I'm not addled, Evelyn." He pretended to think of something else and wrote down her suggestion. Even if the granddaughter knew about them, he was going to say that he'd never been aware of her. It would play well in the papers should someone spill the beans. "I have enough here, I think, to talk to the man about. He'll be happy that we've taken time out of our lives to give him this."

"If he's the sort of man that we hope he is. I don't know, Lloyd. The kids nowadays, they have different rules than we had as newlyweds. I just don't like all this change. Not one bit." Lloyd didn't want to ask her what she meant, but he did. "For all we know, he could care less about what sort of person she is, and marry her despite what we've told him. You know the kind of man I'm talking about. Remember Burgess? He married that tart that he met several years ago. She wasn't any better than a street walker, and he parades her around like she's the queen of the castle."

"Oh yes, I remember her. He said he loved her and that he didn't care that she was penniless. Moron. What sort of person does that when they have enough money to buy any pedigree they want in a woman? For the love of Christ, Evelyn, can you imagine what I would have suffered if you hadn't been as well moneyed as me?"

"Neither of us would have been able to join the club or

go out into public. No, I'm glad that you were very picky about who you married. It's made us the talk of the town." He nodded. "Now, when you meet him, but I'm sure you've thought of this, you want him alone. He might try to bring that woman to your meeting, and that would be horrific."

"Yes, yes, I know." He made a mental note to write that down when she left him. "I don't think I'm going to tell him that you're going to be there either. He might think that if it is the two of us, then he will need to bring her as well. You do want to be there, don't you?"

"Oh yes, very good thought. All right. I would very much like to be there, just to see what transpires. I shall keep my mouth shut, like a good wife, and show him what he is missing if he marries her. Is that all right with you?" He told her it was an excellent idea. "Oh Lloyd, I'm so glad you saw this in the paper. I can't think what would have happened had they sprung this on us like Jewel did about the marriage, then the baby. Oh, my, I don't think I can take much more tonight. I think I shall have a brandy and go to bed."

"Yes, you do that, dear. And while I'm working down here, I'm going to see about what other information I can find. That deal that she has with the city, maybe I can do something to stop that before she drains that poor man dry, as her dad wanted to do to us." Evelyn nodded and toddled out of the room. Lloyd shivered when he thought of the damage he was going to have to clean up after this mess. It was almost more than he wanted to take on.

CHAPTER 7

Jason was gone when she woke. He'd left her a note telling her that he had a meeting this morning with a company about pans, and that he couldn't miss it. She was still pissed off about the engagement announcement in the paper, but he had told her that it wasn't his fault.

"Where did they get this information then, if not from you?" He told her that it could have been any of his brothers, or his dad. "Why would they do that when I've never said I'd marry you? I don't even think you've asked."

"No. I was going to do that today, when I was showing you the house, but I was deterred. You have a very lovely, distractive body." She told him to behave. "I am. I've not ravished you once since we entered the dining room."

He'd taken her then, right there on the dining room table. And then in the bathroom while she'd been showering. The closet when she'd gone in there to see if she could find one of his shirts to wear, then again on the bed. Spencer was worn out and exhausted.

Taking a shower in his bathroom was like heaven. There were sprays at several levels, and a massaging showerhead that rained on her hard, making all her sore muscles feel much better. Dressing was a slight problem, as she had nothing to wear there. Thinking about a simple pair of jeans and a T-shirt, she screamed when they appeared on her body.

"Miss?" She asked Garrett to wait a moment. "Miss, I must know that you're all right. You should come out now before I come in there."

She came out of the closet and stood before him. "I was dressed." He nodded. "No, you don't understand. I was thinking of clothing and it appeared on me. I didn't know that…. Spud, he dressed us yesterday when we were…. He put us some…. I didn't know I could do this."

"Spud is a very powerful watcher, my lady. I would imagine that if you were to ask him about it, he will tell you that he only gave you the power to do so, that you dressed yourself. You must have impressed him mightily if he shared." Spencer didn't know what to say, and it seemed that Garrett understood. "If you would like to come to the kitchen, my lady, we can fix you something to eat. There is still staff that you've not met as yet."

"There is a thing in the paper. Have you guys all seen it yet?" He told her that they had. "I don't know where that came from. Someone did that and didn't ask. I don't even know if I'm marrying Jason. I mean, he's kind of rich, I think. I don't have two pennies to rub together, and he doesn't seem to care."

"Lord Jason wouldn't, my dear. He is very rich, as well as powerful. And I can find out who put the announcement in the paper for you, but I don't think it'll matter now, will it?" She shook her head. "Very good. Also, I'm to tell you that a cell phone is on its way for you today. Lord Jason said that while the two of you can communicate, it will be beneficial that you have a phone in the event of an emergency."

She didn't know if she could get used to this. Not just the house and the staff, but the magic to dress herself. There were other things too that weren't anything that she thought she could get used to. Spencer had money to burn now, according to Jason, though she told him that wasn't her thing. But the family was loud and loving. And she was cared for. She hadn't had that since her dad had died.

The kitchen smelled heavenly, and as soon as she sat down a large plate of food was set in front of her. There was much too much food on the plate. But almost as soon as she took her first bite, she dug in like she was starved.

"Miss, if you don't mind, I do have some things that I would like for you to answer for us." She thought of all the questions that they might have for her and nodded. They were going to ask her what made her think she should be here. Or what she was going to do in the kitchen. All things, she felt, they could say to her. "All right, I have a list here. The first thing on it is, are you allergic to any foods or other items?"

"No, but I can tell you that I don't eat broccoli. I like it, but it just doesn't care for me." He nodded and wrote that down. "Allergies. I do have a sensitivity to Band-Aids. They break me out. All things sticky cause blisters. But I don't think that's what you were talking about, is it?"

"This is useful information to have, ma'am. Do you have any favorite foods? Sweets, perhaps?" She listed what she could think of, which mostly consisted of comfort foods like pork roast and potatoes. Green beans with ham. He wrote everything down. "Now, I'm to ask you about the household. Is there—?"

"Garrett, why do you think I'd have anything to say about this household? This is Jason's home. You work for him, not me." She was calm about the question, while her insides were churning up. "I've never said I was going to live here. And I'm sure that Jason has things just the way he likes them."

"You must, my lady. We need you." She told him that she doubted they needed anyone. "Oh, but we do. Lord Jason is a good man. He had days where we wished him gone for the day, but he is a good man. But since you've been here, and I realize that it's only been two days, but he is a changed man. His mood has much improved, his disposition is so much calmer. It's all better since you've been here."

"And you attribute that to me?" He said that it was her. "I don't see that. I mean, yes, he is different, not the stuck up prick that he was, but that can't be all me."

"Yes, it is." She looked up to see Jason standing in the doorway watching her. He smiled at her when Garrett said he'd return in a moment. "You getting things cleared up?"

"I have no idea. This place is huge, and Garrett is under the assumption that I'm in charge." He kissed her and she felt her body warm to it. Jason sat at the table with her. "Don't get me all worked up, please. I'm sore. And still catching up with how exhausted you made me last night."

"I'm sorry, love. I just find you to be so delicious." She smacked his arm. "I had an interesting call today while I was in the office. I'm not supposed to tell you, but Mr. Wendel Patterson called me. He wanted to set up an appointment for me to meet with his boss. I told him I could meet him tomorrow, but where I wanted to. And that I'd tell him the place later. He's not at all happy about it, but I don't care. I wanted your opinion on this before I go see him."

"And why would that bother me if you were to go see someone?" He told her who the boss was. "I don't know him. Why would he—?" Comprehension washed over her. She shook her head when she realized who it was. "He's my grandfather."

"Yes, you get it now. He only gave me a name and a time that I'm to have lunch with him. So, I did some digging myself and found out that he's your mother's father. Your grandfather, as you said." She asked him what he wanted. "I don't know, love. Perhaps he's decided that you are someone that he wishes to get to know."

"I seriously doubt that. When Dad died, he had all these correspondences in his desk. I'm sure that Dad never meant for me to find them. But there were letters from my grandfather, via his attorney, calling Dad such horrific names and blaming him for my mother's death." Jason asked what she had died from. "There were complications. I was delivered by C-section because, as I said, she'd been hurt somehow at work. There was nothing wrong with me, Dad told me. But the doctor told my dad that she bled out, hemorrhaged. They tried everything to save her, but she was just gone. It broke my dad's heart. Dad loved her…he told me that every day we were together. I also have her diary. She wrote about her love for him, as well as conversations and such that she had with her own dad. Some of the things he said to her were as bad as what were in the letters to my dad. Dates, times, what was said. I don't know why she did that but to read them over. I'm glad that he wasn't in my life. He tried to have Dad sell me to him. To raise me the correct way. Whatever the hell that means."

"Your grandfather sounds like a really nice guy. May I read them? All of it?" She told him he could have them, but asked why. "I think that this man is going to try and tell me

KATHI S. BARTON

that he knew nothing of you. I don't know why he'd care, but that's all I can think of. The announcement in the paper is the only reason I believe he'd do something like that. I just don't understand why he'd want to talk to me, after not having anything to do with you since you were born."

"Me either. I mean, it's not like he wants to give me away or anything. Speaking of which, you've still not asked. I know that it's assumed and all, but, well, I'd like to be asked if I want to marry you. You know, since the entire world knows now." He grinned at her and got down on one knee. "That's not necessary, Jason. All you have to do is ask. There doesn't even have to be a ring."

"Oh, but there is one." He put in it front of her and she could only stare. "Do you like it? It was something that I designed.... Well, I designed it a long time ago."

"For another woman?" He said no, that at one point in his life, he'd been an artist and designed jewelry. "Oh. Well, I didn't want to wear someone else's cast off."

"Never for you. I think, when I designed this, I unknowingly created this just for your finger." She loved that he was romantic right now. "Spencer Jewel Graham, will you be my wife for the rest of our lives together? Will you hold me when I need it? Love me even though you want to bash me over the head? Be a sister and daughter to my family?"

"You mean the rest of my life." He stopped putting the ring on her finger and looked up at her. "I know that I'm only human and that I'll die well before you do. I think that, in a way, is what made me fight falling in love with you. Now that I have you—and yes, love you—I find that I don't want to leave you behind."

"You won't." She asked him what he meant. "As my mate,

as my wife, you'll live as long as I do. You'll have magic, as I do. Perhaps not as strong, but you'll have it. And someday — I'm not sure how that works — but someday, you might even have fangs with which to bite me and feed from me as I do you. But as for leaving me behind, that's not going to happen. You're going to live as long as I do."

"Really?" He nodded, the ring still at the first knuckle on her finger. "What about children? I mean, obviously you can make them, your dad has, but I'm not a vampire."

"You could be, but you can still have children with me. I never thought to ask before. And if you're going to ask me, yes, I'd love to have children with you." She nodded. "Is that a yes to my question, or are you still absorbing?"

"Both. I might have questions later." He said he expected no less. "Then yes, I'll marry you, and all that other crap."

"Such a romantic you are. Well, here's to our crap." The ring fit her. And it was gorgeous on her finger. "Do you like it?"

"Oh yes, it's beautiful." The band was wide, about half an inch of platinum. But the simplicity of it just made the rest of the ring more beautiful. A row of emeralds circled the middle, diamonds on either side of the brilliant green. A Tiffany setting held the biggest diamond she'd ever seen in the middle of the circles of other gems. "This is far too much, Jason. It's beautiful, like I said, but much too pretty for someone like me."

"It pales in comparison to the amount of love I have for you." She stared at him, shocked that he'd say such a thing. "I can see by your face that you didn't think I'd love you, or that I would love you this quickly. But I can tell you that I do. Very much so, and with all of my being."

"Oh, Jason." She wept then. He held her on his lap while she cried out tears of happiness. She'd never in all her life thought that anyone would love her like this. And she loved him as well. Looking up into his face, she told him that. "I love you. As much as, if not more, than you love me."

~~~

Jason was as ready for this meeting as he could be. He'd read over the papers, diaries, and court documents that he had. Christ, this man wasn't at all what he expected when he'd gotten the phone call yesterday. He had made it sound as if by meeting with him, Jason should feel privileged. When in actuality, he felt sickened to the core about the man and his actions regarding his daughter and granddaughter. Not to mention, the man who had loved them both.

To calm himself, he thought of all the lovemaking he and Spencer had had last evening. Taking her to their bedroom, he was glad that Garrett had done as he'd asked. Not that he wouldn't have, not ever, but it looked better than he thought it would when he imagined taking Spencer up there after asking her to marry him.

There were dozens of roses around the room...in vases, petals on the floor, and bed. He'd asked for wine to be chilled, and instead got champagne. A box of chocolates that looked to be about ten pounds, as well as a small box that held the necklace that matched the ring she was wearing. Another one of his designs.

"You've been very busy." He told her she made him want to do this. "I'm glad. It's very unlike you, in that it's very romantic."

Jason picked her up in his arms then, laughing when she did. To have a beautiful woman in his arms, Jason thought there could be nothing better. When he put her upon their bed, he stood over her and stared. She was his. Now and forever.

He made love to her gently, touching her as he stripped off her clothing. Tasting parts of her that he'd neglected before. Or he thought he had. She tasted of heaven, sunshine, and a uniqueness that he couldn't get enough of.

Sliding deep inside her, he felt as if he'd come home, as if his body, not just his heart, had found the one that had been created just for him. Jason loved her more in that moment than he had any other time. And was sure that in the coming decades, he'd love her even more.

"Take me." He licked along her throat, tasting her need like his own. When she begged him again to bite her, Jason felt his cock fill painfully, his body tighten with the urgency to come. And when he sank his teeth into her pounding pulse, he came with her. He cried out around her flesh as he emptied his soul into her. Jason came three more times, each more powerful than the last until he simply passed out.

"Jason?" He looked at the person in his doorway, and it took his befuddled mind a few seconds to remember where he was and that his dad was there. "Are you all right?"

"Yes. I'm in love." Dad laughed and Jason smiled. "I don't think I've said that to anyone before. Just to Spencer, I mean."

"It's a great feeling, being in love. And it will only get better. Children will make it stronger. You do want children, correct?" Jason told him that they did, but had questions. "I would imagine, knowing Spencer, that she has a lot of them. She's a very thorough girl."

He handed his dad the paperwork that he'd gathered, and the diary and notes from Spencer's parents. As he read them over, he did his notes as well which had to do with the pan factory and the new contract that he'd written up for them. They were going to be out of the red soon, with the new revisions that were going on now. But he couldn't concentrate, and put it on the table about the time his dad was finished reading.

"Nasty stuff this man has said to his daughter. And what he wanted from the son-in-law isn't very good either. What do you suppose would have happened to you and Spencer had he gotten ahold of that girl?" Jason said she might have murdered him. "No doubt. You're very lucky in that, I believe."

"She might have been killed by him too. He didn't seem to have much good to say about his own child. A grandchild would have fared no better, I don't think. Dad, what do you think that he wants with me? I've read about the man and the things he did to his daughter and her husband. He isn't someone that I would think would care about Spencer at all." His dad leaned back in the chair across from him. "You think that he wants to hurt her?"

"I think he has already. Though she's not said that, I think when she was able to read about the relationship he had with them, she began to hate him even. Do you think she's figured out that her grandfather is the one that made them broke for the first years of her life? That it wasn't until he gave up on trying to get her that her dad was able to get a job and a home for her?" Jason said that she had. "Poor child. To think that someone that is supposed to love you would treat you that way. He deserves whatever he gets. And on that note, I think you should have Spencer there."

"He might just leave." Dad told him he wouldn't if he

110

didn't know she was there. "You mean compulsion. I don't know, Dad. Do you really think that she needs to hear all the garbage he has to say about what he thinks? The person he is, isn't the man that he shows to the public. Some think he's a bastard, but enough think he's an all right guy."

"Yes. I do. She needs to know the real man. And the only reason you'd use that is to make him not see her and to tell you the truth. You've done it before. You're stronger now, so it wouldn't be a problem. I think it might do her some good to hear all his excuses. If she wants to, that is." Jason asked if he would be there for her as well. "Of course. I can cover myself, and you take care of her. She'll need this, I think. Don't you?"

"Yes. I'm not sure why, but I believe she will. But it'll be up to her." Spencer walked in just as he said that, and asked him what would. "Your grandda. I have that meeting at noon today, and we were just talking about letting you be there."

"He said not to tell me." He explained to her how he could make it so he'd not see her. "Okay. If I were to take something to record him, would he know that? I don't want to do it to give to the police, but there are other means to embarrass him if he's going to get nasty."

"You want to record what he has to say?" Spencer nodded. "No, he won't see anything. You'd have to be quiet and still. I can hold him, but if you start talking or moving around, I might lose the connection to him. You want to?"

"Yes, I do. I really do." Jason looked at his dad while Spencer continued. "And if it won't cause you too much trouble, I really would like to take something to record whatever he has to say. I have no idea why, but I have a feeling that it's going to be enlightening to hear it all. And for posterity, I think we should have a copy of it. In the event he

111

tries something like he did with my parents."

"All right." She looked worried, but he knew that she wanted to do this. "We should leave now, so we can purchase a recorder for you. Using your phone, it might go off or something. This way we have it where we can date and put a time on it. I want to be as assured as you are that we get this right. After today, I don't think he's going to let us in the same room with him, with or without something to record him."

The restaurant that they were going to was a quiet place, with rooms set up for small and large parties. Jason was shown to the one that he'd reserved, and was glad to see that it was done just the way he'd asked. There were cameras already in this room, but he knew that Spencer also needed to do her part. In the event, like she said, he got nasty with them.

Jason was playing this by ear. He'd never done anything remotely like this before. Meeting a man that he didn't know, with no clue as to the reason. The only thing he knew for a certainty was that Mr. Spencer wasn't going to get whatever he wanted. It didn't matter to Jason if he only wanted to smoke a cigarette, Jason was going to tell him no.

While he was waiting, he looked over his notes again. There were several points that he wanted to make, questions that he needed answers for, and a few things he wanted cleared up for Spencer. She'd not asked him to do anything, but he needed to do it for her. Lloyd Spencer and his wife, Evelyn, were going to answer to him.

"They're here. I've asked the hostess to mess around with him a little, to give you time." He nodded at his dad and stood up. Pulling the shadows around Spencer, he told her that he loved her.

"I love you too, but don't kill them. I don't want to have

to visit you in prison." He winked at her. "Why does that not instill comfort in my heart?"

"Such confidence. Dad, did I tell you that she's not a romantic either? Such a worrywart." He turned to the door when it was opened and took the man's hand into his. Reaching to his father, he asked him to do the same to the wife. "You will not lie to me, nor will you see anyone else in this room but myself until I tell you goodbye or allow you to see them. Understood?"

Evelyn sat down and looked around, dazed. Lloyd did as well, but he appeared confused, like he was trying to figure something out. Jason was sure it was because he'd seen his dad and Spencer in the room, but now they were gone. Good, that was just what he wanted. Him to be a little off his game.

"Why did you want to meet me?" Lloyd asked him his name. "You know who I am as well as I do you, Lloyd Spencer. So, again I ask, why did you want to meet me?"

"To give you some information I don't think you have." Jason asked him like what. "That woman that you're thinking of marrying. Did you know that her entire family is nothing but money grubbing killers?"

"You mean her mom, your daughter?" He said that she was the only innocent one in that group. "And what is it that Chad and his daughter, Spencer, took from you? I'm assuming that you've filled out a police report."

"No. I can't.... You're not listening to me. They stole my daughter from me. Then killed her. She wouldn't have died if she hadn't been married to that man. A blue-collar worker? Marrying someone like my only child? It's not what I would have picked for her. And that brat they have. I have no doubt that she's no different than her father. How much has she taken you for?"

"Taken me for? Why, nothing." Lloyd said that she would. "Doubtful. I'd give her anything that she wanted, I love her that much."

"Idiot." Jason asked what he'd called him. "You're an idiot if you think she won't take you for all that you have. She's beneath you. You should know that. Why are you marrying someone so far below you on the food chain? Don't do it, young man. You're going to regret it if you do."

"Are you threatening me?" Lloyd said he wasn't. "It sounded as if you were. Perhaps you should tell me from the beginning why you've asked to meet with me. And no lying to cover your mistakes."

CHAPTER 8

Lloyd was getting frustrated. The man was simply too dense to see he was messing with the order of things. There were rules among their kind, and this young man was ignoring them all. For a piece of ass, he would imagine.

"Look. I'll explain it to you in simple terms. When you marry beneath you, such as you're doing now, you start to weaken the bloodline that makes our kind, the rich, such superior stock." He asked him if that was what his daughter had done. "Yes, that's it exactly. When she decided to lower herself to that man's level, I did everything I could to make her see reason. But nothing, not even taking the one thing away that I knew she valued as much as I do, money, did any good. Then she got pregnant. That should never have happened."

"Perhaps they loved each other. Just as I do your granddaughter." He told him for the fifth time to stop calling her that. "But she was a child of your daughter. That, by law, makes her your granddaughter. Why are you so set against that? Or is it that people will find out? Is that what this is about, you're afraid that people will find out that you have a granddaughter that you never acknowledged or even bothered to see?"

"She's a bastard of that man and my lovely daughter. She

can't be anything to me. Don't you see?" Jason told him that he did not. "Like you've said, what will people think when they figure out that I have a long-lost grandchild? And that my daughter soiled herself with that man? They'll feel sorry for me, of course, but some of them will wonder at my feelings. Not that I have any for this child, but to think that I'd have to associate with her.... Well, that makes my skin crawl. She's lower than either of us."

"You keep saying that. That man, his name was Chad Graham. As I said before, perhaps your daughter loved him. And that alone should be enough for you. But you've never answered my question...why do you care who I marry? Other than you think that my stock, whatever that is, would be corrupted. And when we have children of our own, we'll make you a great grandfather, and your wife a great grandmother."

"Heaven forbid." Evelyn shivered. "I do not want a thing to do with the child either. Nothing, I tell you. And you might not want to count on children, Mr. Crosby. She might have the same thing her mother did."

Lloyd was going to bring that up next, scare the young man into leaving the brat. No children meant that there was no one to carry on the line of his people. And he knew that someone like Crosby would want to have children of his blood to continue the family fortune. Just as he had wanted.

"I'm sorry, what do you mean, the same thing her mother did?" Lloyd looked at his wife, then back at Jason when he continued. "Are you telling me that Jewel shouldn't have been pregnant, and you knew that?"

"Of course we did. We were devastated when the doctor told us that she wasn't perfect. But we figured that we could

116

pawn her off on someone with children already, and no one would be the wiser. But that man, he knocked her up, and we, my wife and I, decided that she'd face the consequences of her actions. We just didn't think she'd die, but the brat would." Jason asked if she could have been saved had she known. "I don't know. We were only told that she should never get pregnant. If he told us that she'd die, then we might have told her. But we were so overwrought that she wasn't perfect, and we missed that part."

Jason stood up and began pacing the room. It was then that Lloyd noticed how tall he was. How in shape the man was. He was going to ask him about the trainer he used, or the drugs, when the man stopped suddenly and looked at him. Lloyd had a feeling that he might have just gotten what he was saying. He had the strangest smile on his face.

"Let me get this straight in my mind. You knowingly allowed your own daughter, your only child, to die because you didn't bother to tell her that she shouldn't have a child? And your excuse was that you thought the child would die and not her. Because, and this is a paraphrased quote from you, you heard that she was imperfect and didn't pay attention to anything else. Is that about right?" Lloyd told him that they didn't mean for her to die, but she needed to learn a lesson in what was the proper order of things. Like dating and marrying someone that wasn't of your kind, like with money. "I'm sure that she did. By dying and leaving behind her own child, that taught them all a lesson, didn't it? And this thing with Spencer, you hope that she has the same 'defect' as you call it, and hope that I'll leave her because of it."

"Yes, that's it. You're getting it. And now that you do, I'd like for you to put a retraction in the paper about your engagement to this person. If too many people believe it, then other children of our kind will think that they can marry whomever they wish. Can you imagine the kind of creatures that would create?" Jason sat down again. He was glad for it…Lloyd was starting to feel dizzy from watching him. "I have a list of other things I should like to go over with you. Things about Graham that you might want to know. It will more than likely show up in the brat. That way, you can have information when the people ask why you've dumped her… and they will."

"I'm not dumping her. Whatever gave you that idea? I've told you repeatedly, I'm in love with her and am going to marry her. As soon as possible." Lloyd asked him why he'd do that, after everything that he'd told him. "Because, as I told you, I'm in love with her. And if she did have anything wrong with her, which wouldn't matter to me either way, then it shouldn't be a concern to you or your wife. Like I said, I love her."

"If she were here right now, I'd blow her brains out to make you see reason." Jason asked him what reason he was going to show by killing her. "I'm sure then that you'd see that her mind is underdeveloped, and that she's just like her father in that. My daughter was brilliant."

"Really? Because from the information that I've found out about her, she was an average person who was in trouble more than she wasn't. That is, until she met and fell in love with Chad. And from all accounts, and I have those by the way, she was extremely happy and so much in love with her husband that people often remarked on how they wished their own marriage was as strong." Lloyd asked him what he was talking about. What accounts? And by who? "Jewel kept a diary. Of conversations with you. Times and dates. Even what was said. Chad did the same after his wife passed away. Letters from your attorney saying that you were glad that your daughter was dead, so she'd not see what a failure he was. And by that, I mean the fact that you fired him, and made sure that he lost everything in the process. It wasn't until Spencer was ten that you decided to leave him alone. I wonder why that is. Or for that matter, why you'd do that to your only living relative from your child."

"I was going to buy her from him, but he'd not sell. And the few times that we tried to take her, to keep her from being like him, he thwarted us. Like he knew we were coming for her. But once she started school, we knew it was much too late for her. She was going to be just like him." Lloyd asked him about the conversations and why he would lie about them. Jason told him he didn't lie. "You can't have had those. My daughter would never do something like that to me. Contrary to what you think, we were a very close family. Until she messed up by going against what I told her to do."

"You mean the daughter that you let die rather than tell her that she had something wrong with her? The daughter that you left to suffer in heartache, and that's what she said it was, heartache that you would treat someone that she loved so badly. And she was worried for her child and how you would treat her. I guess we all got to figure that out." Lloyd told Jason that he was missing the point. "No, I don't think I am. You essentially murdered your daughter, and left a motherless child with her father who couldn't get a job or a place to live until you gave up your demented dream of making her into someone like you. Which I'm happy to say you were thwarted at that as well. You're lucky I don't....

What is the matter with you, that you'd do such a thing?"

"I don't know what you mean. I'm a good man. I have money, a great deal of it, and I'm not a half breed like that thing you're marrying. You should be thanking me for this, not berating me when I only have your best interest at heart. You cannot marry that thing. I...well, I forbid it." Jason stared at him before throwing back his head in laughter. "What are you laughing at?"

"May I introduce you to my lovely bride-to-be, Lloyd?" She was suddenly in the room with them, like she'd been there all along. "Spencer, this is the man responsible for you being in this world. Not that he wanted you here, but you've heard that part."

"I have." Lloyd stood up and looked at the woman in front of him. The picture in the paper had not done her justice. Christ, she looked just like her mother. "So, you're my so-called grandfather. What a major disappointment you are."

"Excuse me? What right do you think you have to even speak to me? You're nothing to me." She told him he had that right. "I want you to quit this sham that you've created by making this young man marry you. I won't have it."

"*You* won't have it? I had no idea you were allowed to have any kind of say over who I marry or not. And you really should watch yourself, mister. I'm in a shitty mood, and you're not helping." His hand slapped her across the face before he could think. But he would do it again for the way she'd spoken to him. When she spit blood on his foot, he drew back to hit her again. The bitch was going to pay for that. But she spoke then, calmly and without the fear he had hoped for. "Do you feel better, Mr. Spencer? Does it make you feel like a big man to have slapped around your granddaughter? As I said, you are a major disappointment to me."

"You are nothing to me." She looked over at Jason, and he did as well. There was a device in his hands, and he had a feeling that it, like this person, had been here for the entire meeting. "I never said you could record me. What do you think you're going to do with that? You think that anyone will care that I've admitted to not wanting this thing in my life? No one will. So you know what, go ahead, do with it what you will. I just don't think anyone will care as much as you might. You're a fool."

Another man appeared. It was like Lloyd had been in a fog all this time, and only now was it clearing. This man, without a doubt, was related to the younger one. Perhaps father? No, much too young for that. Not that it mattered. They were all off their heads if they thought he was going to allow this. Before he could speak, however, the man did.

"Maybe, but they will care to find out that you murdered your own child by neglect. And perhaps there won't be a trial, but there will be people that will see this and want to talk to you about it. I'm betting that none of it will be good, either." He asked the older gentlemen what he was going to do. "I've a really nice following on one of those social network pages. I'm sure that it'll play well there."

"Lloyd, what is going on?" Evelyn came to stand beside him, and he put out his hand to shove her away. Instead, he gripped her hand into his tightly. He felt like a drowning man. "Who are all these other people? I thought you made it clear that we were going to talk to him alone."

"I don't know the man, but that thing there is Jewel's daughter. And she thinks to blackmail me with something that I've said. They don't stand a chance —"

"You think I want to blackmail you? For what, money? I don't want, nor do I need, anything you have. I don't even like the fact that I'm called Spencer. Perhaps I'll just go by my middle name from now on. That should toast your oats." He asked her what she was talking about, Spencer was a good solid name. "Yes, unlike I am, correct? But my middle name is Jewel. I'm going to be called Jewel Crosby from now on. I think I like that. What do you think, Jason?"

"I love it. And you." He wrapped his arms around the woman and pulled her close to him. Hadn't he heard a single thing that he'd said? "How about we go out to lunch? You, me, and Dad."

They started out the door, the three of them. Lloyd just stood there, disbelieving his own eyes on what they were doing. They were going through with this, like he'd not just spent the better part of the afternoon, time that he'd devoted out of his busy day, to help this man. And this was how he repaid him? By doing it anyway? By walking away?

"Come back here right now. This discussion isn't finished. Do you hear me?" He and his wife were the only ones in the room when the door shut. He looked at her. "I have a feeling that we've not heard the last of this. They're going to come running back when people like us find out what they've done. I should just let him suffer, but I think I'll help him when the time comes. He will owe me, but I think we can work something out. Don't you?"

"I just don't understand people, Lloyd. I really don't. It seems the harder we try, the more people push back." She looked at the door. "My goodness, she does look like our Jewel, doesn't she?"

~~~

122

"It's done." Jewel nodded at Crosby. "I'm truly sorry about all this, Jewel. I never dreamed in a million years that Mr. Spencer would have said those things to you."

"Me either. I mean, I did think he was a horrid man, but I never dreamed that he would let my mom die because of some sick sense of hierarchy." Crosby told her that she'd be fine now. "Thank you. And what do you think of my new name? The rest of them just sort of took it in stride, but no one has said anything."

She sort of liked the new name. It was much friendlier than just being called Spencer. Every time she heard it, especially as a child, she'd thought of suspenders. Like those things old men wore to keep their britches up.

"I'm thrilled to death with it, if you want to know the truth of it. To be associated with a person like that can't have been easy for anyone." She agreed. "It's still not too late for me to cancel that video, Jewel. It's going to come down hard on him."

"It will. I know that. And a lot of people might not care, like he said. But if one person out of a hundred does get something from it, like what a monster he is, then that's good enough for me." Crosby sat down and asked her if she was all right. "He hoped for me to die, that whatever was wrong with my mom would kill me. He didn't even think about how it would affect her, so long as she learned something from it."

"Sadly, there are a great many people more like him than there are good ones like you." She thanked him. "All right then. We have things to settle, you and me. I believe the last time we played you beat me twice. So, to my way of thinking, you owe me a match. What do you say?"

They were into their second hot game when Jason joined

them. He told them not to stop on his account, that he had work to do anyway. Crosby was a good player, better than anyone she had played before, but he joked more than he thought about his next move. Which gave her an advantage every time. By the time he left she was feeling better, but not over this shit yet.

"How did it go?" She told Jason that she'd beat him once and lost once. "Good. It's good that you let him win once or twice. My dad is a sore loser. Did he tell you that the video is uploaded?"

"Yes. But we sort of avoided talking about it after that. How many people have viewed it?" Instead of answering her, he turned the computer toward her and she looked twice before she spoke. "That can't be right. Five million views and ten thousand shares? Are you sure? He just put it on there."

"Dad knows the key words to use to make people want to look at it. You remember, he's been around longer than me." Jewel nodded. "There are comments to it too. Would you like to see them?"

"I'm not sure. Do I?" He told her he'd only read the positive ones, and only a few of those. "Are there a lot of negative comments?"

"Two that I've found so far. One of them said that the camera shook too much, and the other one was upset that Mr. Spencer wasn't arrested on sight." He laughed when she asked him if he was serious. "I am, very much so. A lot of people feel the same way, saying that he should have been taken to jail, or at the very least questioned about her death. A few hundred people wanted to know if they could help you out as a witness. And if you can believe this, a couple of the board of directors from his company have called me twice to see if this is real or not. I told them it was very real."

"What do they care? I mean, this was just personal on my part. His too, I guess." Jason explained it to her. "You mean they could take his company away from him because he's a bad representation of it? I guess I can see that. But I never meant for him to lose his job."

"He'd lose his company too, and his shares along with it. I mean, you do have to answer to directors when you have them. They might not own the majority of the stock, but they can all vote you out if they find that you're not up to the standards or rules that were set when you hired them. It happened once when I was doing that sort of thing, working in the corporate world. It's one of the main reasons that I do what I want when I want now. I have no one to answer to."

"What do you do?" He told her that he did everything. "I don't understand. I mean, I know that you've been around for a long time. Your dad said he'd been a doctor for a while. Sean told me that he'd been a teacher, and a botanist. What kind of things, other than being a corporate guy, have you done?"

"When we were first given this gift, I did whatever I could to be outside. I was a landscaper. I rode the high seas. I even, for a few years, was a farmer. I didn't care for that overly much. It's hard work, and there is so much to fail. I don't care for that." She told him she'd noticed that about him. "Thank you. Then as the years went on, I started looking around for something where I could use my mind as well as my body. It was hard, back then, to hide from people when you were going to outlive them, especially as we never age. So I started looking for ways for our kind to be able to reinvent themselves after a time. It paid well, and I learned a great deal about mankind. Some not so good."

"You became a forger?" He laughed and told her that it was necessary back then. "Why not now? I mean, it seems to me that a lot of people would notice you more. With the cameras on their cell phones. Plus, all those cameras on the buildings. I would think that you'd be more inclined to be seen rather than not."

"No one cares. And if they do care, they usually have their heads too buried in the cell phones that you mentioned to see what is right in front of them. And even if someone were to notice that they knew me a long time ago and that I look the same, they usually just don't say anything for fear of being wrong. Or worse, offending me and me shooting them for it. There is a great deal of that going on as well." She got up and went to sit on his lap, a place that she had come to call her comfort zone. "Are you all right, love?"

"I think so. I'm better now that you're home. So, back to my question, what do you do now? I'm assuming that it's lucrative." He laughed and asked her if she was going to try and spend all their money. "No. I don't even know how much you're worth. Not to mention, I don't care to shop or do any of those girly things. Just curious, and wanting to not think about my grandparents and the type of people that they are."

"All right. You and I are worth more money than we could ever spend, even living forever. Billions and billions of dollars. And I make more all the time." She stared at him. "We not only have money, we have homes, cars, and antiques. Also, businesses and even jewels…not as lovely as you, but we have them. As for what I do, I run several very well established companies. Take on smaller ones that I might see a spark of something in and help them get up and going.

Much like I'm doing with the bag idea that you had. Or the pans company we were working on before."

"Pan company? I'm assuming that they make pots and pans, and not like Peter in the story." He laughed and she smiled at him. "What is it they do?"

"Canada Pans. And yes, they make baking pans. But up until we talked to them, only two different kinds. Their business was going to fail, and it was a good company. So, I went in and told them that in order to stay in the market, they needed to expand their line. Just one to start, and that would bring in enough business to not only upgrade their building, which it needs, but they could tweak their lines to make a variety of different designs." Jewel told him that her dad had one of them. "I can tell you right now, as soon as they come out, I'm going to buy a few. They're high quality workmanship. Something that I look for. Like your bag idea."

"I so wanted that to work." He told her that it was. Her building was being renovated right now. "You really are doing it? I thought that after...Well, I didn't know you were...."

"You thought what?" She felt her face heat up. "What did you think I was going to do, Jewel? Get you in my home then let you think I was doing it to appease you? I don't work that way. If I say I'll do it, then I will."

"I have other ideas, projects that I'd like to work on. I mean, they're not all mine, but things that I've heard people want to try and sell. Prototypes of other people's work. I found that I'm very good at that, taking an idea and making it tangible. That is where I found most of the mistakes in the gift bags. By making them, and then having to ditch the ideas for one reason or another." Jason asked her if she wanted a place to work on them. "You mean, like an office? Or a warehouse?

I suppose one day I'd like that, but not yet. I might be a failure at it."

"I doubt that. You did an excellent job on presenting your idea to us, too. I was impressed, even though I was a dick about it. And you were...let's call it forceful when you knew that the deadline was about to expire on it and made us, or me, pay attention to you. That is wholly my fault. I've been, I guess, distracted." She told him he was a bastard about it. "Okay, a bastard. But you did well. Maybe that could be a part of your services. Being the front man for small companies that need help. I can train you on what to say to banks and investors."

He showed her which buildings they owned, as well as some of the houses that were in other countries, on the internet. Jason told her about each one of them, how old they were. Something that he knew about them, and how when he'd been on the crew of some of the houses, he had planted the very trees that were as tall as the homes. It was well after midnight when they finally went up to bed.

"Something that I've been meaning to ask you about." She yawned as she continued. "I can dress myself. I mean, not like I can pull on my clothing, but I can think of an outfit and I have it on."

"I'm glad. But can you strip as easily?" Laughing, she tested his question. "Yes, this will be so much nicer, I think. You only need to think of being naked for me, and I can take you wherever we are. Yes, this is a very good bit of magic that you have, my love."

Suddenly she wasn't so tired.

JASON

CHAPTER 9

Jason loved making love to Spen...Jewel. She was much like her name in her giving to him. He never had to say anything, she was simply there for him. As he touched her nipple and watched it tighten, just for him, he had to smile. Something as innocent as her body reacting to his touch made him feel like the greatest man on earth.

"You're teasing me." He told her he knew that, it was part of the fun. "Not for me it's not. It's like you're taking your pleasure and making me suffer. How about if I did that to you?"

"You mean tease me? Honey, you do that with every breath you take. Every time you come into a room where there are other people, and I can't just throw you upon the table or desk, or even the floor, and have my way with you. That, my dearest love, is the ultimate form of torture for me." Her smile lit up the room. And when she pulled him down to her mouth, he kissed her because he loved her, taking as well as giving as much as she wanted. "I love you, Jewel. So very much."

He touched his mouth to her pulse, could almost taste the blood flowing beneath her flesh. Moaning his name, she told him to bite her, to give her the pleasure that she wanted.

Sinking his fangs into her, he felt her richness fill him in ways that no one had ever done before. Her life-giving blood, even for him, was more than he had ever thought he'd have in any lifetime.

Entering her, filling her with his body, was no less powerful. She was his, forever. As he made love to her, holding her, touching her to make her moan, sigh, or even just to smile at him, Jason felt as if he'd been given a gift like no other. Even the gift of sunlight and all that it had been for him and his family was nothing compared to making love to this woman. And when she cried out, her body bowing up off the bed, wrapping around him, he felt the bed tremor with the power of it.

"Again." Jewel shook her head, told him she was spent. "But I'm not finished yet, love. I need for you to be so exhausted and satisfied that you never want to leave me."

"Never. I'd die without you." He took her harder, her words giving him something more, something spectacular. "I'm coming."

He bit her on the shoulder this time, feeling her tongue lick along his own pulse. And when she sank her teeth into his throat, tearing into him like he had her, he came. His body cried out with the pain of it, and the pleasure.

When he woke, it was late afternoon. He wasn't sure why he'd slept so long...perhaps Jewel had worn him out more than he'd thought. But when he turned on the water to the shower, he found a note on the counter from her.

I've gone into town with your dad. I got a call from the contractor that said that there was a slight problem with the north wall. Who knows? Anyway, contact me or buzz me – whatever it's called – when you get up. Then she signed it, *Love, Jewel.*

130

Smiling, he stepped under the spray as he reached out to her. He felt like something was blocking him, and wondered if she was having trouble with it again. For some reason, she could stop people from getting in, and he'd yet to figure out why. As he finished up in the bathroom, he reached for his dad.

As soon as he got the same block, he began to worry. Not just a little either. Something was wrong. His dad wouldn't block him, not when he was with Jewel. He knew of her sometimes inability to get it right the first time. Trying not to panic, he reached for his brothers, all of them, to find out what they knew. Elliot was the first to answer.

I haven't seen Dad today, nor Jewel. I thought they were there at the house. He told him what he'd gotten from Jewel. The silence at the other end had him running down the stairs to leave the house. *I'm at the site now, Jason. There isn't anything wrong with it. And I just asked Howard, and he said he didn't call anyone. Nor has he seen them at all today. You need to come here. Right now.*

In minutes he was at the site. He might have been there sooner, but he had to inform Garrett what was going on. Garrett told him that Jewel had left the house with his dad around nine that morning, and didn't seem to be distracted or anything. It was after one now, which meant that she'd been missing for over four hours.

No one at the site had called, not even to check on them. And no one else had seen either of them around the area. Jason continued reaching out to both his dad and Jewel, but kept hitting the wall. He knew they were alive, because if they were dead, he'd hit a void. Hitting the wall, no matter how scary it was, kept him from going into full panic mood.

"Her grandfather, do you know where he is?" Jason looked at Grayson. "Jason, think. Do you know where Mr. Spencer is? Where he might be?"

"No. I mean.... Do you think he might have taken her and Dad?" Grayson said he might have, but the only way to find out was to go to their house. This time they drove instead of using their power. As nervous as they all were, there was no telling where they might turn up. Jason tried to wrap his mind around the idea that Lloyd would have hurt her and his dad. He'd been mad, yes, but would he go to such lengths to make him not marry her? If so, he was dead wrong. "Do you think that he took her to teach me a lesson?"

"I don't know. But I do have an in at the Spencer Corporation. The board of directors met last night and voted him out. He was informed of that early this morning. He also lost his shares due to the fact that they're claiming that his committing murder gives them the right to take them from him. According to my source, he didn't take it all that well. Threatening to have everyone fired if they did this. It was a done deal before they even notified him, I guess." Jason knew it was going to hit him hard, and was glad for it. "How do you want to play this, Jason? You want him dead or answers?"

"I want both." Grayson said it wouldn't work that way. "I know, but if he's in on this, if he's hurt either of them, he's as good as dead. I'm in love with Jewel. And Dad is all we have. I want answers, but if I don't like them...well, if I don't get answers, then all bets are off, as humans are so fond of saying."

"You got that right." They pulled up in front of the house and looked around. "The last time someone was here, there were people all over the place. It looks dead around here. You don't suppose he skipped town with her, do you?"

"Please. Don't use that term. I don't want to think of them dead." Grayson said he was sorry and they got out of the car. "This is very strange. By now, there should have been someone coming out of the house. I mean, that's what Dad said when he came by with you the other day to see about information on the Spencer Building that we're working on. A butler came out to greet him. And there wasn't anyone at the front gate just now, now that I think about it."

"They were all over us." Grayson laughed as he continued. "Do you suppose they saw the recording too and walked out? I would have. Christ, this is much better than I thought it would go over. Not the part about our family, but the way this man is going down for crimes that he committed."

Knocking on the door, they could hear someone on the other side. Grayson knocked again, harder this time, and Jason looked around. There was something decidedly wrong here. It was too quiet. Not even a lawn mower running. When the door opened finally, he stepped back when he saw Evelyn standing there with a gun in her hand and her hair and dress unkempt.

"What do you want?" Gone was the mealy-mouthed woman from the other day. This version of Mrs. Spencer, Jason would bet, was her truer form. "My husband isn't here right now. And even if he was, you'd not be welcome. This is all your fault. Our underlings quit, I have no one to help around here, and I can't find anyone to fix my hair. You go away and marry that bitch, see if we care."

"Underlings?" Grayson looked at him when she nodded. "They call their staff underlings? Christ, no wonder they walked. I would too."

133

"We paid them. And they had a good job. We never demanded more than they could give us. It's not our fault that they're of inferior bloodline and stock. It's their duty to want to serve people like us, and they should have been grateful that we even hired them to touch our things in the first place." Grayson laughed and she pointed the gun at him. "You should be ashamed of yourself, coming into our lives and making things go wrong. You have to fix this. I don't know how, but this is all your fault, and that other person."

"He had nothing to do with what is going on in your life. Neither of us did. You did that all on your own. Where is Jewel?" She told him that she was dead, and he felt his knees weaken before she continued. "If you mean that upstart of yours, you should keep a better leash on your animals. And I will not use my little girl's name to call that thing. I've told you before, get away from here. I don't have anything that belongs to you."

When she stepped back, likely to slam the door in their faces, the gun went off and splintered the wood just above his head. He looked at Grayson, just to see if he'd been hurt. He was nursing the knuckles of his right hand. It occurred to him then that his brother had hit the woman, and she'd not fallen as he'd thought.

"You hit her?" Grayson nodded and smiled at him. "You told me to behave myself, yet you were allowed to hit her? How fair is that?"

"She was calling my sister an animal. And I thought if I hit her before you tore her throat out, we'd save time by not having to go to jail." Jason thanked him. "We'll look around here and see what we can find while Sean and the rest of them look around town. I know for a fact that Lloyd owns three buildings in the downtown area. Or he did. I think they were also under the umbrella of the corporation."

They went through the entire house after securing Evelyn to a chair with some tape. There were several other guns in the house, and they hid those too. Neither of them wanted her to get free and shoot them. There was no sign of either their dad or Jewel, but he did find some records in Lloyd's office.

"It's about us." He looked them over quickly before handing them to his brother. "And these are older files that talk about his daughter and Chad. He must have had someone watching them every second of every day they were together." He handed those to Grayson too, not bothering with them for now.

"It says here that he did fire Chad when he found out that he was married to his daughter. He even tried to get their marriage annulled, stating that his daughter was just a female and not of sound mind. I'm glad to see that someone had the sense to have that thrown out in court." Grayson laughed. "Jason, he didn't change his will."

"So? Unless it says there where they are, then I don't really care." He told him he should. "Why?"

"Because per this will, his daughter was to inherit his estate, in the event that he ever retired or died. I'm assuming that he thought he was going to live forever. Anyway, and in turn, any children of his daughter would inherit if he outlived her, or she could take the company when he was no longer an active participant to it. I'm betting that in all the scheming and planning their demise, he forgot about that. Jewel, your mate, is a very wealthy woman." Jason asked him why that mattered to what was going on now. "I would think a great deal. He's lost his business. But before he lost it, he had retired.

Completely. He only got information once a month about how well it was doing. His granddaughter should have been running the company. She'll take it over as soon as this mess is done, because she should have been running it the day that he left it for greener pastures. And that will put a damper on his saying she wasn't worthy of marrying you."

"But we have to find her first." As soon as the words left his mouth, the front door opened. They'd stashed Evelyn in the kitchen, as she had awakened and was making too much noise. Jason stood up when he heard Lloyd call out to his wife.

"Evelyn, where are you? I need to tell you what has transpired. Evelyn?" Grayson stepped into the front hall when Jason did. Lloyd turned and looked at them, and Jason could smell the blood. He was hurt. "What are you doing in my household? Get out this minute, before I call the police."

"Go ahead. And while you're at it, tell them that you've kidnapped my future wife, as well as our dad. I'm sure that it'll go over well." Jason took a step toward him and smelled only his blood, and not that of Jewel or Dad. "Did my dad rough you up a bit? I'm betting that he got in a few kicks before you were able to subdue him."

"She did this; the upstart fights like a man. Another reason for you not to marry her, she's not a female that behaves when her superiors are speaking to her. What did she think she was doing, trying to tear my eyes out?" Jason laughed and so did Grayson as Lloyd continued. "I did ask her nicely to get into the trunk, but she went crazy, telling me that she was going to hurt me. Well, she did. And don't think I'm not going to sue her for this too. You never answered me, what are you doing in my house?"

"I do believe that she was going for your throat and not

your eyes. She's vicious like that. It's what I would do." Jason moved closer…he needed to touch the man to sort through his memories. "When I find her, and I will, you are going to prison. For a very long time."

"Jason, I've called the police, they're on their way. I explained how the missus tried to kill us and we tied her up. And that Lloyd here admitted to taking our family." He nodded at Grayson but kept his eyes on Lloyd. "Don't kill him."

"I don't plan on it. Not now. I want him to suffer for his actions." He touched his finger to Lloyd's head and found not only where they were, but what he'd done to them when he'd gotten them in the sublevels of the basement. "Grayson, there is a bomb set to go off in eighteen minutes at the building on Main and Gorsuch. Four-twenty-four is the building number. Will you stay here? I need to go."

"Yes, go. I'll wait for the police and tell them what else is going on. Give her my love when you find them." He used his considerable power to take him to the site where they were. But just before he was going inside to get them out, the building blew, knocking him back on his ass, and then he was out.

~~~

"Jewel? Jewel, honey, where are you?" Her head was pounding, but she knew that she had to get to Crosby as he called out to her again. "Jewel?"

"I'm here." He asked her if she was all right. "I don't know. I've never hurt in so many places before. Are you all right?"

"Yes, though I'm beat to crap, but all right. I'm coming to you. Don't move." She wasn't sure that she could. There was a large piece of concrete on her, she'd just discovered. Jewel looked up just as a shadow moved over her. "There you are. Can you move your arms? Legs?"

"Not my leg. It's penned under something." He nodded and started to lift the large stone that was over her. Her scream had him stopping, and she was sick with the pain. "Please, just leave it. It hurts too much."

"I can't leave you here like this. I have to pull this off to make sure that you're not bleeding to death under this thing. I can smell the blood, Jewel. You're hurting badly." She nodded and told him she was sick. "I'm sure you are, love. I'm sure of it. When I move this, you're going to pass out. Might be the best thing for you if you just let it take you."

"I felt Jason. As soon as we got out of the basement, I felt him. Now I can't. Was he here too?" Crosby closed his eyes for a moment, then looked at her. "Please don't tell me if he's gone. I don't think I care to know that just yet."

"He's alive. Hurt, but I've called in the rest of them. They're on their way." Jewel cried, it was such a relief to know that he wasn't dead. "Now, I have to move this, Jewel. As soon as I do, like I said, you're going to hurt more. Just let yourself go and I'll make sure you're all right."

The big piece of concrete was lifted off her legs and she screamed. Jewel knew that she was broken, that there wasn't any way for her to get up and walk away from this. As Crosby held her hand, telling her that she was going to be just fine, she cried.

"You go ahead and cry, Jewel. I would be too if I was hurting as much as you are." She asked him if Lloyd had gotten out. "I don't think he was here. It was his plan, I think, to make sure you and I were killed in this."

"I got you hurt in doing this to him. Making him admit that he'd hurt my family." He asked her how she'd come to that conclusion. "If I hadn't come to this family, you'd be going on with life and nothing would have happened to you."

"Now you listen here. You gave me something no one has before. A reason to get up and get going. I was so close to ending my life. The boys, they were sick of hearing me complain all the time. Telling them how I was wronged in saving the queen. I wanted to join their mom, so badly that I couldn't see what I had right in front of me. You showed me that when you fell in love with my Jason. And my other sons, they love you just as much as I do." Jewel cried a little more. "The day that you came to the family, that very day I had purchased me a gun. I was going to put it to my heart and kill myself. It's the only way, I think, other than to cut my head off. And I didn't know how to make that work or I would have done it. I didn't because of you, Jewel. Because of what you gave me. My life back."

"Thank you." It was getting harder and harder to keep her eyes open. "Will you go and see about Jason for me? I'd feel better knowing that he's all right too."

"I'm staying right here with you. Those boys, they'll bring him along soon enough. You just hang on for a little while longer." She looked up at him and could almost feel the fear that was on his face. "You just hang on and don't go to sleep. I need you here with me."

Jewel had a feeling that she was going to die. She could no longer feel her legs, and her arms were getting too heavy to hold up. Laying her head back, she felt cold and started to shiver. The pain that she was in, it no longer hurt as badly as it had before. Crosby started talking then, but she couldn't understand his words. It was too much. Her body, she knew, was closing down, and she was going to die.

She'd gotten them out of the building, but not far enough. Crosby was too weak, he told her, or he'd just take her out with him. And no matter what she told him, he just wouldn't go and save himself. They both knew that if they paused, even for a few minutes, they'd be dead. The timer on the bomb was close to one minute when they found it. The countdown was moving faster than they were. Running for all they were worth, she felt the explosion just as she was pulled from the building by Crosby.

"Spencer Jewel Crosby?" She looked at the woman in front of her when she said her full name. "Hello, my child. I see you've gotten yourself harmed. That will not do."

"I don't hurt." She said that she knew that. "Crosby, he is here. Did you come to see him?"

"No. I've come to see about you. Crosby called to me. He is a friend of mine. It has been a great many years since I saw him, but you, it's you that I wanted to see." She nodded and felt her belly churn up. "I'm going to touch you now. And when you wake the next time, you'll be with me, in my home."

"I thought it burned down." She told her that it was a new one. "You're her, then. Aren't you? You're the faerie queen, Kilian."

"I am. And Jason has been good to us over the years, and I should like to return his kindness." Kilian told her to close her eyes.

"I'm dying, aren't I?" She told her that she was. "I don't want to, but I know that it's a part of life. My grandfather did this to us. If you don't mind, instead of helping me, would you make sure that Crosby is all right? He's such a good man. And I love him like my own dad."

"Such selflessness. Jason is the same. You are a perfect pair." She loved that, but knew that she was going to leave him alone now. "He has taken care that we have plenty of flowers to use. And to eat. I have spoken to Spud, who has done nothing but sing your praises since you helped Fairaday with the cleaning of her trees. I have moved her, just as I am you. She will reside and care for the trees on your land, so that she might be close to you and your home. Thank you for the warning, Jewel. It might have ended badly for her should you not have told them of the impending destruction to the area."

"Remind Jason to put out trash cans for her, ones that don't lock." She said she'd do that. "And to put out a salt block when they need it so that she can use the droppings. I no longer hurt, my lady. I'll be dead soon, and I won't worry so much if you ask Jason to do those things for me."

"I will, my child. You must rest now." Jewel's heart ached with the pain of missing Jason. "Rest, and when you wake...."

Kilian was still speaking when Jewel felt her life drain away. Nothing hurt...the darkness didn't just take her, but seemed to wrap her up in a warm blanket and hold her. Jewel felt the rest of her close down, even her heart. She was going to miss Jason so very much, but at least she knew that he was going to be safe.

141

JASON

CHAPTER 10

Jason woke and tried to sit up, but the pain took his breath away. He looked at his dad when he pushed him back to the bed, and let him. He mentioned Jewel's name, but he was still fighting the pain and couldn't quite understand what he was saying. Then he simply blacked out again.

When he woke the next time, he lay very still. There was a light on, very dim, and his brother Ryan was sitting in the big chair reading a book. He said his name and he got up and moved closer to him. With Ryan sitting in the chair closest to the bed, Jason asked how Jewel was.

"I don't know. I mean, I know that she's alive, but we haven't been able to see her." He asked him why the fuck not. "Take it down a notch, Jason. She's with the queen."

"Kilian?" Ryan nodded and sat back in the chair. "What happened? I know that the building blew up. Did she not make it out?"

"According to Dad, they were both out, thanks to her. But not far enough to escape some of the debris that hit them. He was weak, but able to heal. She'd kept his beast under control by telling him to get his ass in gear. I think that is a direct quote. Anyway, they didn't get far enough out of the way, like I said, before it went off. They had some time, but not enough,

143

I heard. They were talking when Kilian showed up. Dad said that Jewel was near death when Kilian took her." Jason sat up but didn't stand...he was very weak. "She touched you as well. When you hit your head...Jason, you were nearly dead as well when I reached you. Kilian said that I was to sit with you until Spud or someone came to me. Then they'd take you here. Jason, your skull was split all the way open, and I saw your brain."

"I don't remember any of that. The pain, but nothing more." Ryan told him he'd never forget it. "I'm so sorry. I'm glad that you were there for me, but I have to see Jewel. I need to know that she's going to be all right."

"Fairaday was here a little while ago. She's been checking on you every couple of hours since you were brought home. By the way, the Spencers are gone. When the building exploded, the police sort of lost track of them in the rush to get downtown, and we've been looking for them. Not all of us; we've also been taking turns sitting with you." Ryan took Jason's hand in his. "You scared us all, Jason. And Dad was nearly having a breakdown when you were brought in here. Don't do that again."

"I'll try my best not to." He had to lay down again and close his eyes. "When she comes back to check on me, wake me, please? I need to find out about Jewel."

"All right. But I have let the others know that you're awake and seemingly all right. You know your name and Jewel's, and that was better than any of us were hoping for." Jason smiled. "Good thing you're hardheaded."

Jason drifted in and out. He saw each of his brothers at least once, and his dad several times. When he woke again and could see well enough to make out the painting across the room, he sat up carefully, then and remained still. Dizziness swamped him, but not like it had before. Standing up, careful not to wake Elliot, he made his way to the bathroom.

Turning on the light so he could see himself, Jason winced at how he looked. There were cuts all over his face, and one of them looked deep. There were some bruises too, but nothing that wouldn't heal when he fed next. Looking at the stall, he thought about taking a shower when the door opened after a short knock.

"No showering alone. I know that you'd feel better, but you lost a great deal of blood. Enough that you won't heal." He asked about Fairaday. "She has been by, but she wouldn't allow us to wake you. She said that Jewel is still resting, and you'd do her no good if you were with her. Rest is the best thing for you both. Also, I'm to tell you that when Jewel wakes, you'll be the first that she tells. But until then, we were told to assume that she was resting, as you should be doing."

"Yes, I understand, but it's hard to rest when all I want to do is see about Jewel. Have you heard anything about either of the Spencers?" Ryan told him all he'd heard was that there was a statewide man hunt for the Spencers, and no trail leading them to their whereabouts. "He tried to kill her and Dad. I don't.... Why? Over some money? Christ."

"The police have been by a couple of times. Mostly to check up on you. They talk to Dad about what they've been able to piece together. The Spencers are broke as far as they know. If they had a stash, they cleaned up after themselves after getting into it. As of right now, they've got roads and airports on high alert, as well as bus stations. I don't think they'd go that route, but who knows what desperate people will do." Jason staggered back to the bed with the help of his brother. "I wish that I could feed you. You're too weak to do much of anything."

"Jewel is the only one that I want to heal me. I need her." Ryan said he could understand that. "I don't suppose you know how to contact anyone to find out about her, do you?"

"No. I mean other than to go in the backyard and yell out her name, I haven't any idea. Dad claims that all he did to get Kilian to come to him in the first place was dig into the dirt around them and beg for her help. For Jewel, not him." Jason sat there quietly and let his head settle. It was pounding, but he told Ryan to go on. "She transported her, Dad said. Just touched her arm and they both disappeared. I think she came upon you first, that's why we were told to wait with you. And since then, we've only gotten information, but no contact with either Jewel or Kilian."

"How long have I been down?" Ryan pulled out his phone and looked at it. "I'm assuming that it's been more than a few hours."

"Yes. Six days. It's Wednesday, and you were hurt on Thursday of last week." No wonder he was so weak. He'd been out for a long time. "I've been keeping up with your projects. I hope you don't mind. And the building for Jewel's Bags is doing very well. Construction is moving along nicely. And applications to work in it are coming in from the site I set up. There is a lot of talk about what is going to be made there, but no one knows for sure. I've not said anything because it's sort of fun to let them keep guessing."

"You think of the name?" He told him Dad had. "I like it. Simple. I bet that Jewel will as well. I just wish she was here so I could see her. I miss her a great deal."

Jason must have dozed again, because when he opened

his eyes, Kilian was with him. She was a beautiful woman, even with the scar on her face from the burn from long ago. He asked her how Jewel was.

"Much better. Still in a deep sleep, however. She was hurt badly, and without the magic of my home, she would not have survived." Jason thanked her. "No need for that, my friend. I owe you more than I can ever repay. You are doing well, too?"

"I think so. I'm weak, but don't feel too bad." She nodded and moved closer to him, sitting on the bed. "You saved our lives, didn't you?"

"No more so than you have mine, daily. I know what you've done to ensure that we're not harmed again, Jason. You are too good a man to let die because of the actions of someone as bad as the Spencers." He thought about the magic that he'd surrounded her with. And that he reinforced all the time. "How much does it cost you, to do something so wonderful?"

"Nothing compared to what the world would be like without you and your kind here. I am only making sure that you're around for my children." She nodded and touched her fingers to his forehead. When he looked around, he knew that he was no longer in his home. "Where is she?"

"You must be quiet." He said that he would. "She is in the chamber beyond, but I must warn you, Jason, she was severely injured, and we had to do things to keep her alive."

"Magic." She told him yes, that was some of it. "I don't care, Kilian. I really don't. So long as she's with me and alive, then I don't care if she's just like you."

"That is precisely what she is." He paused in going to the chamber and looked at the queen. "It was either change her into a magical being or lose her. It's why she is taking so long to heal. Not just because of her injuries, but also the magic is taking over her body. Making her like me. You as well, but you weren't dying when the process started. We could give it to you in small amounts, and we have. Thusly, it didn't take as long. Fairaday brought it to you daily."

"I'm no longer a vampire." She said that he was. He was all things. "You mean a shifter? I'm a shifter?"

"You are all things, Jason. Magic is yours for the taking. Not just mine, but all magic. You and Jewel, you will be in my shadow." He looked confused. "No, not shadow. You will be my family. I don't think I'm explaining this very well. Here, let me show you."

This time when she touched his head, he felt like he was being squeezed through a sifter. He saw shapes and images, memories that were not his own. Spells and how to make them. Words that would work magic as well. He looked at Kilian when things started to settle.

"There were others. Other magical beings that helped save us. I know them all." She smiled and said that he would. "What am I going to do with all this knowledge, Kilian? This is more than I need to heal."

"You will rule." He was sure that he'd misunderstood her, and turned when he heard his name. Moving toward Spud, he turned back to ask Kilian what she'd meant, but she was gone. Going into the room, he decided to ask her about it when he saw her next.

~~~

Jewel didn't move, but looked around the area in front of her. It was sort of freaking her out a little. There were... she thought they were faeries and other tiny little creatures, but she wasn't sure. For all she knew, she was dead and these were a part of her afterlife. The movement at her waist had her looking down at the large hand that wrapped around her.

"How are you?" Jason. He kissed her on the ear and she turned to look at him. "Are you really awake this time, or will you fall back to sleep in a few seconds?"

"I don't know. How many times have I done that?" He told her a few. "I think I'm aware. Have I ever said that before?"

"No. You just grunted and rolled over the other times. How are you feeling?" She rolled to her back and saw more of the tiny people on the ceiling. Jason looked where she was. "Their magic is what kept you alive. I guess they can just be together in a room and their magic is powerful. They've been in since I have."

"How long have I been here?" He said ten days. "Ten? Really? I actually thought that I was dead when I woke just now."

"Yes, you have said that when you were out." He pulled her closer to his body and she snuggled under his chin. Then she snapped her head back and looked up at him. "What is it? What?"

"Your dad. He was hurt. Where is he? Is he all right? I need to see him. I need to—"

He put his hand over her mouth and she looked up at him. "He's fine. Better than we were. Right now, he's at his home fielding off the newspaper people about the trial that is going to be set soon. They found your grandparents and they're in jail."

"He took us. Lloyd grabbed me and your father and made us get into his trunk." Jason said that he knew a little from his dad. "He hit him first. I have no idea why he did that. I would have gone with him had he just left him alone. But as soon as he hurt your dad, I went a little nuts. I think I hurt him more than I might have before meeting you."

"Lloyd hasn't admitted to anything yet. All he is saying now is that he was framed, and that no one said we could record him that day. Even though it has been pointed out, several times, that at the end of it, he says he doesn't care. Evelyn has been quiet for the most part. She's going to have a few more charges against her than Lloyd will." She asked him if what she'd done was what put him in jail. "You mean the filming? No. I mean, part of it, but mostly it was about you and Dad."

"He was insane. Telling me that he had to teach you a lesson. Kept asking why he had to be the one that enforced the rules, while everyone around him was well aware of how things should go." Jason asked her if she'd tried to contact him when she'd been taken. "No. I know that I should have, but in all that was going on, I completely forgot until we were running out of the building. But before then, I don't know that I could have. We were in the sublevels and surrounded by stone."

"Dad told us that you saved him. That had you not talked to him, keeping him calm, he would have let his beast go and gotten shot. I guess that your grandfather held you at gunpoint for a few hours." She asked him not to call that man her grandfather. "All right. But you should know that there are other things going on that will need for you to acknowledge him as your relative. But we can talk about that later. Dad said that you were lured to the job site, but were run off the road."

"Yes. By the way, your dad is a terrible driver. I thought at first that he'd run us off the road again, but he bumped his head. Then I saw the men...four of them. They dragged your dad out just as he was coming around. That's when they hit him. I think they meant to kill him, but he's not human and I don't believe they were aware of that." Jason told her that few were. "So, they had us in the trunk of a car. I hit my head a couple of times, so I had no idea where we were or how long we'd been in it. Your dad was still out when they took us in the building and tied us up."

She thought about what they had said to her, the men. How they were going to get her after Lloyd was finished with her. It was just what she deserved, they said, for her trying to be something she wasn't. Jewel had an idea what they were thinking they were going to do to her, but she wouldn't go down easy. They would regret touching her family. Then Lloyd had showed up. Jewel told Jason what he'd said.

~~~

"You have to call and get that video taken off the internet. Today. You're making things very difficult for me. Even my company has kicked me to the curb." She told him good. "No, you don't understand. I need that company. You can't get it because you're never going to amount to anything. You should know your place and stay in it. This going around trying to make yourself look better, it just won't work. Anyone like me can tell when someone is faking their superiority. Especially you."

"Usually when someone wants something from someone they're nicer about it. Not insulting, as you're being." He asked her what she thought he'd insulted her about. "You saying that you're better than me. That's not a way to get things done for you. Not that I would anyway, but I so won't do it now."

"But I am better than you. I have a lineage that goes back for generations. There is no working class or your kind in my family, and there never will be. You are a disgrace to me and my kind. Now, as I was saying, you will call those people up and tell them that you've made a mistake, which won't be hard to convince them of since you're just white trash. And make them take it down." She told him no. "Am I going to have to go through this all again with you? You have no right to tell me no. I'm far superior to you, and you will abide by my rules. You're no better than the underlings that work for me in my home."

"You call your staff underlings?" He told her that was what they were. "It's small wonder that they've not poisoned you. Or at the very least, spit in your food. Not that it should surprise me what you might call them, but I am surprised that they stayed with you all this time. You're an asshole."

"I most certainly am not. And they would never dare to do that." She had only nodded at him. "I shall bring you a phone and you can make it go away now. To be honest, I was surprised that you even knew of such things. I thought that only smart people could do things like that."

"I have a master's in business management, you fucking dick. I graduated at the top of my class with a four point three average." He just shook his head at her. "Let me go and I'll show you what else I learned in college. Self-defense classes were offered, and who knew that I'd have to use them on an old fuck like you? Let me go, you narcissistic prick."

"Gutter language. And I no more believe that you have a high school education than I do you having a college one. Do you have any idea how easy it is for people like you to get a piece of paper printed up with whatever you want? I bet you never thought that I'd know that, did you? But you will curb your language. I'll not tolerate that." She told Jason that she had laughed. There wasn't any way this man was going to think she was anything but a money grubbing person, as he accused her dad of being. "Now, what do you need to make this work for me?"

"Your head blown off? Perhaps a knife in your heart? Or better yet, you could go fuck yourself." Lloyd had slapped her and she pulled her arm free of the tape. She thought he was just as surprised as she was when that happened, but she reacted quicker.

~~~

"I punched him in the face, just as I pulled my other arm free, then my legs. Then I beat him for ten minutes, ten glorious minutes, before I was shocked with a Taser. The last thing I saw before passing out was him all bloody." She looked at Jason when he laughed. "I wasn't terrified as much as I was pissed off."

"He's still sporting a few bumps and bruises. Lloyd told the police that he'd fallen a few times trying to get away from someone. But it was obvious, Dad told me, that they were made by you. I tell you, I've never been so proud of you than when he told me that." She looked at her hand and noticed that there wasn't a mark. Thinking that he'd healed her, she listened to him tell her about the other things that had been going on. "Evelyn is in jail as well. Attempted murder. She fired at one of the officers when they were at the house, too. Also for your kidnapping, as well as my dad's. Plus, the attempted murder of you two, since she knew about it, when the building was blown. There will be a lot of lawsuits from that one because of the amount of damage done to the buildings closest to it. Even if he wasn't in enough trouble over this, he compounded it by trying to harm you guys."

"There were four men with us. Henchmen, your dad called them. I didn't see them when we were getting out of the building. So, I'm assuming that they left when Lloyd did. Do you know where they are? I'd like to teach them a few lessons on my own." He told her that they'd been dealt with. "Do I want to know?"

"No, you do not." Jewel was afraid he was right. "And there is something else. There is some paperwork that you need to take care of as soon as we're home. There is a clause in the ownership of the firm that Lloyd owns. If he were to retire, which he did, then the company would go to his daughter. If she was unwilling or unable to run the firm, then any children of hers would take it over. That would be you."

"No." He nodded. "But I don't want it. I mean, he hates me. Why would he leave that in his will?"

"Grayson seems to think that he might have forgotten about it, or just never figured he'd die. Something about the wording made him think that your grandfather thought about never dying. I think it was just a typo, but a funny one." She was still thinking about Lloyd's firm as Jason continued. "I've bought the shares."

"I'm sorry, what?" He told her that he'd bought up the shares that had been put on the market when things started to go in the dumpster. The board had decided, for obvious reasons, to get out while the getting was good. "So, what does that mean? I mean, other than you probably spent too much."

"I never spend too much. And I got them for a song

because your grand — Lloyd has made an ass of himself and the prices dropped considerably." She still didn't understand and asked him about it. "Lloyd owned fifty-two percent of his firm. Evelyn owned five percent. So together they owned more than half the stocks. The board of directors owned the other forty-three percent. But they were the ones that ran the company in his absence because his daughter is deceased and you were an unknown. When the business was thriving, which it was, it was worth about four hundred dollars a share. Now, after this hit the papers and the Spencers were arrested, it dropped to about six dollars a share. Some of the board members sold most if not all their stocks. With the stock that you will get now that you're a part of this, and what we were able to purchase for nearly nothing, we own eighty-five percent of the company."

"But it's not worth anything." He told her it wasn't worth anything yet. "So, you're saying that we will make it viable again."

"No, you will. I think, with your understanding of products and clean air workings, that you could make the company more than viable, and quite productive with products that everyone can feel good about using. You'd make it a force to be reckoned with. And, there just happens to be a paper mill in the company that you can use to start things moving in that direction almost immediately." She told him she wasn't sure that she could do that alone. "Are you asking me to help you? Because, I would gladly, help you with everything."

She got up and moved around the room, touching the flowers that were in vases, a book that was open on a stand. Jewel wasn't thinking about what she was seeing, because her brain was working hard to muddle through what she'd just been told.

"What does the firm do? I mean, other than make money usually." Jason told her they printed two newspapers that were failing. "And this is what I'd turn to make my bags? That's where the mill comes in."

"Yes. There are other things as well. One is a bakery. You don't make the bread there, but you own a percentage of what the people who make the pastries earn. Too much, if you ask me, but I didn't make their contract. Also, there is a manufacturing company that used to make rugs. So far, all I can find out about that is that the work is now done overseas and the building is closed. It did employ over two hundred people when it was running." She asked him to give her a minute. "I love you, Jewel."

She turned to look at him. There was too much going on in her head at the moment, so she just stood there, letting it settle around her. Looking around, she saw that the room was now empty of the little people and they were alone in the big room. It occurred to her that she had no idea where she was.

"Whose house is this? And for that matter, why was it filled with the little people? Where the hell are we?" A woman walked in; her face was familiar, but she didn't know her. "I remember you. You were...you were there when I was dying."

"Yes. I'm Kilian. I brought you to my home when there wasn't any way for me to save you both. You've been our guest for a while now, and I'm so glad that you are well." She sat down, and it was perhaps the most graceful thing Jewel had ever witnessed. "I have some important things to tell you both. Some you may like, others I'm thinking not very much. I changed you in order to save you."

"Into what?" Kilian smiled and offered her a seat. "I'm just fine right here. What did you change us into? I'm assuming both of us, since we're both here."

"Yes, you're both now what I am." Jewel sat then, right on the floor. "I can see that you're taking this very well indeed." The laughter was like bells blowing in a gentle wind. Then Jewel fainted.

CHAPTER 11

Jason just watched her. Jewel had been pacing the hallway for the last ten minutes. He didn't know what was going on in her head...he'd tried looking, but it was a jumble of thoughts and he left it alone. She'd get through this, he had no doubt. Just as she had at Kilian's home.

She'd woken, after only a few seconds, and asked Kilian about a thousand questions, but there were more. Both of them were still a little in the dark about a lot that had been done to them. But for now, they had to deal with the board of directors.

When Elliot came out of the elevator, she went to him and hugged him. The rest were coming too, with Dad, and that was what they were waiting on, he told his brother when he asked.

"Here is what I could find out about each of the men on the board." She nodded and took the file, and then handed it to Jason. Elliot turned to him to tell him what he'd found. "There are some pretty shady dealings going on with this group. More than we thought."

"And bank records are here as well?" Elliot said that he'd also been able to find a couple offshore accounts. And informed him that they'd been emptied as of an hour ago.

"Thank you. We're going to go in when Dad and the others get here. The meeting started about ten minutes ago."

"Dad was pulling in when I was getting out of my car, so it shouldn't be too long. He's with the others."

The elevator opened and they stepped out of the yawning hole. The secretary that had shown them where the meeting was didn't look up. He'd made sure that the men in the other room had no idea what was going on either. As far as she knew, it was just him, waiting on someone in the other room to come out.

They had a plan. A good one, but he knew as well as his brothers that plenty could go wrong. Someone could be vindictive and have brought a gun. Or they could have changed the contract, without telling Lloyd. Many things could turn the wrong way and this would be all for naught.

He was going in first, then Jewel was going to be right behind him. His brothers and Dad were bringing up the rear, as sort of the heavies. Jason had a feeling that this wouldn't go over too badly. They had covered all the what-ifs earlier, and thought they had it all down. Hopefully. Like he'd told his family, a great deal relied on the board being too set in their ways, like Lloyd had been, to have done much to prevent this. Not that he cared. He had plenty of money to do whatever it was that she wanted, and she was just strong enough to make it work for her.

"Jewel, are you ready?" She nodded, then shook her head. "That's my girl. Come on now, the sooner we can get this finished, the faster we can go to the jail and tell Lloyd what you've done to your company."

She grinned. "He is going to be so pissed off when he finds out that white trash will be taking over his business.

I can't wait to tell him to his face." He took her hand in his. "Thank you for this. I don't know what I'd have done if you'd not been there for me, your whole family hadn't been there with me through the entire process."

"They love you too." She kissed his hand and straightened up her blouse. "You ready now? If so, let's kick some ass."

Elliot and Chase opened the doors for them and he walked into the meeting. The men around the long table were talking about Lloyd, which he figured would be the topic of discussion, what with all the media coverage that he'd been getting of late. And him being in jail wasn't something that they'd be able to not talk about.

The man at the head of the table turned to look at them. "This is a closed meeting. I don't know how you got in here, but I have to ask you to leave before I call security." Jason told him to go ahead, that before he was finished they'd need them. "I'm afraid you're going to have to leave here now, sir. As I said, this is a closed —"

Jewel moved around him and he wanted to hug her. She'd told him all along that she'd not be able to do this, that he'd have to take over for her. Agreeing with her, saying that he'd take over if needed but that she could do this, had fallen on deaf ears. He was glad to see her taking the steps to become the boss.

"I'm Spencer Jewel Graham Crosby. I know it's a mouthful, but that's what you needed to hear. My mother was Jewel Spencer Graham." The man that had told him to leave just stared at her. "You have ten minutes to vacate the building. You can take your coats and briefcases when you go, but everything will be checked before —"

"What is the meaning of this?" Jewel asked for the

161

paperwork and Jason handed it to her. "What is this?"

"The top paper is the contract that you signed when you were brought in as board members. There is a copy of that for each of you. The second is a highlight of the part we're going to go over today. And the last thing is my birth certificate. It states that I'm the daughter of Jewel Spencer Graham and Chad Richard Graham."

The man that had spoken first asked her what that had to do with her interrupting their meeting. It was Jason's turn.

"As of nine o'clock this morning, Jewel Crosby took controlling interest in her company. And in doing so, she has decided to disband the sitting board. If, and I do hope you do this, you decide to fight her on it, there are any number of reasons that we can and will have you arrested." The man huffed. Jason looked at the first sheet of paper with the information that had been found yesterday. "Who is James Sheppard?"

"I am." The man at the head of the table stood up. "And whatever fabrications that you've got in that file won't stand up in court."

"I think they will. You've been skimming money from the two open accounts for the newspaper factory that hasn't processed a paper in over ten years. We've been able to find nearly eight million in offshore accounts that have your name on them. The bank was very helpful in not only assuring us that you opened and authorized them to send the money, but we were told that the money came directly from those accounts monthly." Jason said the next name and that man stood up. "Carl, you have been taking money from the petty cash for eight years. Whenever it gets low, which by your own records is weekly, you have Benson White put more in the account directly from the Spencers' own personal account. Which I'm to understand all of you use from time to time, going so far as to have credit cards put in your name from the account, as well as signature cards so that you can withdraw from it too."

"Mr. Spencer is aware of the things we do here. We sent him the meeting notes and paperwork each month about our balance sheet." Jason handed Mr. Sheppard a sheet of paper that had the notes on it that he sent to his boss. "So, this proves what I just told you."

"Perhaps, if he was still in charge. Which, per the paperwork that my wife handed you, is no longer valid. Mr. Spencer was taken out of the picture the day that he retired. You should have been reporting to his daughter. And in her absence, Jewel. I'm sorry guys, but you are now unemployed."

They were still going on about how they couldn't do that when security came in. The attorney for the company arrived a short time later, and he too was escorted out. By the time they were done for the morning, seven employees remained in the building, and they might be leaving as well. No one, it seemed, was without fault.

"Now to see Lloyd." He nodded and asked Jewel if she was all right. "I am, actually. I didn't think I could do it, but those men really pissed me off. I'm not sure I could have done this a month ago, but right now, I'm thinking I can even run this company. At least as well as Lloyd did."

"I have no doubt whatsoever. The pack that is on our land has been hired to come in and clean out desks of personal property. Then it will be sent to each person, minus things that were bought with company funds. I'm sure that very little will be going to them." She nodded and sat down at the big desk that would eventually be hers when she moved in. "You did really well in there, Jewel. Those men didn't know what to think when you started talking."

"I was terrified. But all I could think about was what my dad would have done. He would have gone in there with guns blazing. Not real guns, but metaphorically." He moved to where she was sitting and picked her up. Sitting in the chair with her on his lap, he held her. "I needed this. How did you know?"

"I didn't. I needed it as well." She sat there quietly, and he held her. There were things he could tell her, plans that he'd made out in the wee hours of the morning, but for now, they were content to sit there. When his dad reached out to him, he asked if she was all right.

Better than all right, I think. She seems to think she can do this. A damned sight better than Lloyd did anyway. Dad laughed. *She didn't bat an eye when she told them that she was my wife. I have things set up for us to get married at the courthouse sometime soon. That's all she wants in the way of a wedding. Not that I blame her much. She'll be the center of attention soon enough.*

I figured as much. But you should be aware that Garrett is planning a little get together at your house too. I'm to call him when I find out a date. He called me just yesterday with the plans. He thanked his dad. *I'm still here should either of you need me. The others, the rest of them, have gone back to their work. I think they had as much fun as they've had in a long while.*

I noticed that. Jewel looked at him and he smiled. *I think she's ready to go see Lloyd now. Are you going to go with us?*

You're damned right I'm going. I cannot wait to see that man's face when he figures out that things aren't the way he likes them. Oh, before I forget. I did what you asked me about the headstone for her daddy. And I might have had it spruced up around both those graves too. Sad state of affairs when you see how young those two were when they died. He asked his dad if he was still sorry for saving the faeries all those decades ago. *No, but I am sorry about driving you guys insane with my whining all the time. I knew I was doing it, but I really did feel like I needed to be with your mom. But Jewel, she's brought me around.*

She has me too. Dad laughed and said that he'd noticed that as well. *I'll meet you in the lobby in a little bit. I'm sure she wants to get this over with.*

"Are you ready to go?" He nodded and asked her if she was. "No, I don't think so, but I'm also looking forward to this. Like I want to rub it in his face that a Graham is running his business even after all he did. Will he be charged with murder, do you think?"

"I would think so. Chase has been looking into the records at the doctor's office. Not officially, but he has had a good look at them. The Spencers both signed the sheet of paper that stated that they had been told about the birth defect that their daughter had. It wasn't found until she was older, of course, but her womb hadn't developed correctly. And carrying a child would mean a death sentence for both the child and mother." She got up and went to the little fridge, which was full of liquor and other snacks, and pulled out a bottle of water for them both. "I think, with the right kind of equipment and knowledge about her condition, she could have been saved. Both of you. And you might have been able to have siblings."

"I'm glad that they're being taken care of...the Spencers, I mean. They killed their daughter, just as simple as that. Like you said, if she'd known then things might have turned out a lot differently." He told her that it was her company. "You said you'd help me."

"I will, but I have several others that I run as well. You'll do fine. And I've moved a crew into the newspaper plant to retool it for printing on the bags you are making as well. The other plant, you can do what you want with it, but I'd put in another one of your earth saving ideas. I know you have plenty of those." She nodded. "Good. Then let's go and see the old man and get this done."

"When this is done, I mean today, do you think we could take a trip? I don't care if it's to the mall, but just us, together." He told her his plans for the day were open, but they could go and get married if she wanted. "Thank you, yes. The sooner we're married, the better I'll like that. I love you, Jason Crosby."

"I love you as well." He held her hand in his and decided that he was going to take her on a nice long trip. One that showed her what money could get you. Then he'd bring her home and see about making a child together. He told his dad that today was going to be the big day.

~~~

Lloyd hated wearing the cheap cotton jumpsuit that they'd given him. It didn't coordinate with anything that was in his little cell. And the itchy blankets were giving him a rash on his bottom. And he did not want to think about the food they'd been bringing him.

Yesterday for lunch he'd had a sandwich. A bag of chips that were too salty, as well as a soft drink. He didn't drink those at all...it was too lower class in his opinion. And the sandwich had been made on white bread. Only poor people ate that, everyone who was anyone knew that.

He eyed today's breakfast tray that was still laying

untouched on the floor. If the black brew in the plastic cup was anything like yesterdays', it tasted like bile. And no amount of sugar would make it taste any better. When he'd tried it yesterday, with his dinner tray, he nearly didn't make it to his commode. Vile stuff, no matter what it had been called. The rest of his dinner was unrecognizable to him, so he didn't eat any of it but the green beans. Which were mushy and too fatty, but he ate them down, gagging on each bite. And there had been two more slices of white bread with butter.

Lloyd heard the door open at the other end and sat still on his cot. He'd been told that if he made any more unnecessary noise he'd be put in a cell that had no windows, and nothing for him to use but a bucket in the corner. He wasn't sure that was legal, but since he couldn't contact his lawyer, he had decided to be quiet. For now, anyway.

The woman and the two men coming toward him looked familiar. He thought it was his attorney with his secretary and some flunky that he'd not bother with, but couldn't be sure until they were in front of his cell. Standing, he looked at them all and tried to think why they'd be there. They were the direct cause of all his woes.

"I've taken the company. All of it, and have fired your board members as of an hour ago." He asked her what she was talking about. "Spencer Corporation is now mine. Well, mine and Jason's, but we went in today and fired most of the people working there. Took over the building and are, as we speak, having it cleaned from top to bottom. I want to start fresh."

"You can't do that. Why would you even say something like that to me? They brought me here under false pretenses, and now you're here talking to me as if I might care what spews from your mouth. Go away. And call my attorney. He'll straighten this out. I'm not supposed to be in a jail with commoners." He looked at Jason when the girl wouldn't stop laughing. "Have you called off this sham of an engagement? I certainly hope you have. I'd hate to think what your parents would say if they knew what you were dating."

"I haven't. As a matter of fact, we're getting married this afternoon. Right after we leave you. Jewel wanted you to know that your business is in good hands with her. And my dad loves her like a daughter. Just ask him for yourself. He's right here." Lloyd could not believe this man and ignored the older man. If he was allowing this to happen, then he too was beneath him. "Did you know that your board members were robbing you? That some of them had offshore accounts filled with your cash?"

"I suppose she told you that." Jason told him that as a matter of fact, she had found it. "Of course she did. And I'm supposing that she knew all about lawyers and such. We both know that her kind can't afford a good attorney. Much less one that can think himself out of a courtroom. No, I won't believe it."

"Suit yourself. Oh, and your attorney, he's been fired too. I would imagine that in a few days you're going to get notified of his loss of license as well." He refused to listen to anything else either of them might say to him. No one of her breed would speak to him like this. Lloyd looked at Jason again.

"My wife. They said that she's been arrested. Can you tell me who would do such a thing? She's delicate." Jason told him what had happened. "And they arrested her for trying to save her home? What is this world coming to? Our kind just does not go to jail. It's not the way things are. My goodness, we don't follow the same laws that the poor does, don't you know that?"

"You think you're above the law?" Lloyd told him that was correct. "You're not. I don't know why you'd think you are, but you have to follow the same rules as everyone else."

"No, no that's not right. We have money…the rules only apply to those people who can't afford to buy themselves out of trouble. And I can. I will, as a matter of fact, as soon as I'm out of here." Jason said there was going to be a trial. "For what? I didn't do anything wrong. Not one thing."

"What about your daughter? Or how about the fact that you kidnapped my wife? Or the fact that you planted a bomb in the building she and my dad were in? Those are just a few of the things that are going to be brought up at your trial." Lloyd just shook his head. This man did not deserve to be wealthy if he was going to be constantly thinking he was less than he was. Someone needed to teach this Crosby person a lesson…the entire family, as a matter of fact. "Do you have anything to say to me about that?"

"Your father is alive, isn't he? And this thing…well, I tried to help you out by killing her off. As for my daughter, I do feel badly about that, but not enough that I'd be put in jail for— That's it, isn't it?" Jason asked him what. "They've put me in here not for her murder, as they've called it, but because they're afraid that I'll try to commit suicide because of it. I won't. I have no reason to feel sad for her passing. She was being taught a lesson, and that is one of the consequences of not knowing your place in the world."

"You're a sick fuck, did anyone ever tell you that before?" Lloyd saw no reason to justify that with an answer. It was, as far as he was concerned, only showing her trashiness. Her tawdry background. "You have no feelings whatsoever that your own daughter died. That she was happily married to my dad, and together they had me. Your only living relative."

"You are not a part of my family." He was getting frustrated again and rubbed the pain between his eyes. "Why don't you just go back to whatever hovel you crawled out of and leave us decent people to our own? You've caused enough trouble, and I for one will be glad never to see you again."

"You won't. But I might send you information on my business, formerly known as Spencer Corporation, now called Crosby Industries." He could not believe that this girl was thinking herself capable of taking over his company. Not to mention, her convoluted ideas that she was on the same level as he was when it came to being an upstanding human. "What? Nothing to say?"

"I'm done trying to tell you that you're nothing more than a product of a good woman and a piece of dung. Your father should have known better than to think that I'd ever allow him to be a part of my family. Do you have any idea how hard it's been on us to keep all that out of the papers? And when she died, well, I can tell you right now, had I been able to, I would have put you in the dirt right alongside her and your father."

"That's quite enough." Lloyd looked at Jason, could hear the anger in his voice. "You've spewed your rhetoric enough to her, and I won't allow you to hurt her again."

"Hurt her? Why, she's nothing. Not even a blip on our kind. She should be serving me, not going around pretending to be something that she's not. You should be thanking me—"

His head hurt...exploding pain behind his eyes took

him to his knees. Something was in him; he could feel the movement of something horrible in his brain. Holding onto his head, he screamed out with the pain, saw blood pool at his feet.

Lloyd could hear someone calling his name, telling him that help was coming, but it hurt too bad for him to answer. He pulled on his ears, hoping to give whatever was there a place to escape. His mind was buzzing, even his body began to shake.

"Make it stop. Make it stop." He felt one of his ears pull free, the pain of it momentarily taking the place of the worm pain…that's what it had to be, a worm in his head. No relief… giving it someplace to go other than his brain did nothing, and he yanked all the harder on his other ear.

Grabbing his hair, he pulled at it. Anything, he thought, he'd do anything to get the pain to stop. Handfuls of hair fell into his blood. He could no longer see; the warm seeping blood was blinding him to everything. The sound of chains, the door opening, had him wiping at his face and he saw her, his daughter, standing in front of him.

"You had to die. You had soiled yourself for anyone, and you had to die. Stop this, Jewel, stop this right now and go away." She said something, her words hard to understand with all the pain. Reaching out to her, grabbing her leg, he told her again that she had to die. "You were dead to me the moment that they told us you were imperfect. You had no right to be born defective like you were."

The pain in his arm had him lashing out. He touched something hard and curled his fingers around it. Pulling it free of its confinement, he knew it was a gun and fired it twice at his daughter. If she was dead, then he would be all right.

But the pain was more, bigger than before. Putting the gun under his chin, he knew the only way to end it was to kill it, and he fired, bursting into tears when even that didn't take it all away.

CHAPTER 12

Jewel watched the men working on the lines. They were set to go soon now…all the components of what she needed for it to work were perfect in the old building. As the lines were turned on, she saw Jason and smiled. She was sure it was the first one she'd had since yesterday afternoon.

"They said that it would work perfectly now that they've replaced all the belts and oiled it up." He nodded and pulled one of the sample pages off the conveyor belt. "I was sad when I saw this. To think that the last paper printed here was the day after I was born."

He put it down and turned to look at her. She didn't want to hear whatever it was that he thought she needed to know. Not today. She went on about the lines, where she was going to put key people, as well as how the cleaning was coming along.

"I have to talk to you." She told him that he didn't, not really. "Okay, but you should know that I talked to Kilian. She was sad that you didn't come with me, but understood. Have you heard anything more?"

"Yes, but I don't want to talk about it right now, okay?" He nodded and followed her to the foreman's office. "Did she have anything to do with what happened in the jail cell? Not

173

that I'm upset, but I'd like to know."

"No, she had nothing to do with it." Jewel was relieved, but the alterative was that she or Jason had done it. "None of us did, Jewel. He did it all on his own."

"He kept saying that I needed to die. I know he meant my mom, but still.... Anyway, what did she say about the magic? I know that you said you'd ask her about it." He sat down and she moved to the other chair. "The products are going to arrive tomorrow or the next day. I have sixty people coming in for interviews, and then after that, we'll have a training class. I don't think the job is too stressful, so I think I'm going to hire a few people from the adult living center. It's the cleaning up that has us so far behind. There are decades of dust and other crap lying around that needs to be taken care of. Some of the windows need replacing as well."

"I heard. Dad said he was out there this morning, and they're all excited about getting their hands dirty. And for such a good product." Jewel told him about the three businesses that were interested in it when they started production. "I've looked over the contract that you had made up. It looks good. I'm glad that you're starting out this way, slowly and without much in the way of added pressure on you or the lines that you are starting up. It'll be smoother running for you."

"Okay, I'm ready for some of it. You said that you talked to Kilian. Is whatever happened to us in her home permanent?" He said that it was. "Okay, so what is it we have? I mean, I know there is something different about me, and the way she talked about it, it was going to be easy to use and to hide."

"She's here. And would like to speak to you. Like I said, she does know why you didn't come with me, but she said she wants to make sure that you're all right." Jewel said nothing.

"She cares."

"I know. But it's so hard for me.... No one has ever cared for me the way you guys do. My dad did, and I thought when he died that I'd be all alone in this world, that no one would ever love me." Jason got up and pulled her into his arms while she sobbed. "I keep going back and forth on whether or not I want to talk about him."

"That's understandable. And you should know that there are a lot of people, not just my family, that care for you." She nodded and looked up at him. "Are you okay to talk to her?"

"Yes, I guess."

He nodded and turned her around, and there she stood. Jewel went to her and was wrapped into her warm embrace and cried harder. As she stood there, leaning on the queen of all faeries, she realized that another woman had never held her this way in all her life.

"Are you all right?" She said that she was, just so emotional. "Yes, I would think that has a little to do with the magic that you have. Not all, but some. You've also had a rough few days."

"I would like to skip over that, if you don't mind. I keep drifting back to the subject, but I don't want to think about it anymore today, if I can." Kilian smiled at her. "You said you wanted to talk to me about the magic."

"I do. I should like to start this by saying that when you were injured in that building, you were as close to death as you could have been. Had I not taken you when I did, neither of you would have survived. I was able to keep Jason from dying, but you, you had to be brought to my home so that all magic could heal you." Jewel told her that she thought only her leg had been crushed. "A spike had gone through your leg and severed the artery there. Had you been in a hospital setting, even with as much of Jason's blood that was in your body, you would not have lived. Your blood was draining out of you quickly."

"I didn't know." Kilian nodded. "And you took me to your home. I know you told us this the other day, but I was too overwhelmed to let it sink in. And then all this other stuff has happened. I, of course, have no memory of any of that, but Crosby did tell me that I was with him, then gone."

"Yes. I had to move quickly. And in doing that, I called to all of earth's creatures to come to my aide. Jason, too, needed more power, and they helped him at his home. After taking you, I used everything I had to give you enough magic to heal first. The rest, it came from everyone that could come." Jewel said she'd like to thank them all. "You are. With your projects here that make things cleaner for us. And so you know, your projects, all of them, will also be instilled with a little of you. Your magic will make the person who buys your items happier, as well as the receiver. The flowers that will be planted with these bags will feed a great many creatures. The earth will benefit from the bounty of the plants and the nutrition that is planted with them. What you're about to set upon, it will be welcomed by many, but help so many more."

"When I started out with this, not just the bags but a few other projects that I had going, it was to make my little world a little better. I never dreamed, not when I first started, that I'd have a way of producing so many at once. Nor did I think that anyone would buy them on the scale that I'm hearing now." Kilian nodded. "This is much bigger than just a few flowers in the ground. It's a way to make everywhere a little better."

"It is. And I'm to understand that you have other projects, not just your own, that you're going to help produce. These will be the perfect things to save the world from complete destruction." Jewel smiled, but she was embarrassed a little. "I'm very proud of you, Jewel. Very much so. Now, what questions do you have for me?"

"What other magic can we do? I'm assuming there is more to this than just a little happiness for someone." Kilian laughed and Jewel smiled. "You have such lovely laughter. Every time I hear it, I think of bells."

"Thank you. I think that is where it came from, bells. Yes, you can do other magic. Shifting for one thing. Both you and Jason will be able to take on the characteristics of anything you've ever touched. Your sense of smell will be stronger, and you will retain that scent in your body for future use. You'll be able to find things with a touch, you'll be able to talk to other creatures, and you'll be far safer when it comes to someone trying to harm you." She thought of the bells comment, but let it go when Kilian started talking again. "You and Jason will be able to speak to nature. The soil, water, as well as the air. Not only that, but control it somewhat if need be. Your children will be just like you two. Magical and strong. I have given some to the others, but not nearly as much as the two of you have. They'll be safe beyond anything that could harm them from now on."

"Why? Why is it you think that we're going to need all of this? And especially me? I'm nothing more than a human who happens to be in love with a vampire. Who has a few ideas that might make your world a little better." She looked at Jason and he smiled at her. "I do love him, but I think, for me at least, I'm not the type of person that deserves such things."

"Oh, but you are, my dear. For the very reason that you just said. A human that cares enough about her world to do something productive about it. You say that you will make our world a little better? You will make a difference in that other people, humans and other creatures, will think that they can help too. Every time a flower is planted and cared for, another animal in my world is saved. Each time someone bends to pick up a scrap of paper, no matter if it was theirs or not, a bit of the earth is saved. When there is less waste on this earth, even with something as small as one of your bags, you have done more than your part in keeping all of us safe." Kilian put out her hands, and there in her palms were trees growing. "Watch what it is that you can accomplish now."

Leaves as green as the grass were filling the branches. The water that was nearby had fish splashing around, the flowers under the tree were stretching to the sun. There was a little trash flying through the air, and as she watched, a small child snatched it up and threw it in the trash can nearby.

"I did this?" Kilian said that she would do so much more too. "I would love to. I would very much like to help you all."

"And so you shall." The magic burned at her fingertips. She looked at Kilian and she smiled. "Let it go, Jewel. Let it go and watch it make a difference."

Lifting her hands up, she felt it roll over her body. As soon as Jason wrapped his arms around her waist, seemingly to hold her in place, she knew that they were combining their strength, and whatever was coming, it was going to be powerful and epic. As soon as she felt whatever she was doing was ready, she pushed her hands up, releasing whatever had been coming, and she cried out in pleasure as she saw it.

It was rainbows and stars. Puppies and kittens. There were colors everywhere. The sound of music...no, it was bells, and birds chirping all around her. Closing her eyes to the dizzying kaleidoscope of things, she leaned back on Jason and let it flow around her. When she was finished, or the magic that she'd released was gone, Jewel felt her body go limp as she smiled. It was finished.

~~~

Jason woke to the most incredible pleasure he'd ever felt. Opening his eyes when his body seemed to come apart, he held onto Jewel as she rode his cock. Christ, he thought, this was a way to wake up. Rolling her to her back, he kissed her, taking his time with his tongue. Jewel yanked his head from hers.

"I need to come." He laughed and she yanked harder on his hair. "Seriously, you need to let me come or I'll hurt you. Then when I've had my pleasure, I'll take your cock into my mouth and suck you dry."

He rolled to his back again and let her have her way. "You do know that 'suck you dry' is my line." She laughed as she rolled her hips slower now. "Do you have any idea what it's like to wake up with you doing all these delicious things to me?"

"No, but you can show me sometime. Your cock was just standing there, and I was so wet that I thought I'd take what I could." He shifted, bringing his hips upward to her downward stroke. "That's it. You're so hard and thick. I think I could do this all day and not ever be bored. Sore, but not bored."

"I thought you were going to come so you could take me into your mouth." He didn't care either way...watching her

179

was as much fun and as exciting as taking her was. "To watch you here and now, it's more than my body can take."

"You can take it because I need you to. Now hush, you're messing up my concentration." Putting his hands on her hips, he let her ride him. "Jason, I want to come so badly. Help me."

Sitting up, he took her breast into his mouth and nibbled on the tip until her rhythm was completely off. Her hands curled into his hair, holding him to her as she moaned. Sliding his hand between then, he pinched her clit and she screamed.

Her release tingled along his own body. As her nails dug deeply into his flesh, he took her throat to his mouth and bit down. Rolling over so that he was deep inside of her, he took her hard as Jewel wrapped her legs around his hips. Sucking hard on her throat, he cried out when she bit him, sinking her teeth into his shoulder so that he saw stars. Emptying into her, filling her with all that he was, Jason fell upon her and couldn't move. He wasn't even sure that he could breathe.

"I think you killed me." She laughed, then moaned. "No more, please. I seriously think that you've killed me. Christ, that was amazing."

They lay there for several minutes. It might have been an hour; at some point, he fell asleep and woke with her still cradled in his arms. He knew she was awake, so didn't speak until she did.

"What we did yesterday, did you know that we could do that?" He told her that he hadn't. "We repaired the building from top to bottom. Fresh paint, new windows. Even the lines are working at top speed."

"I heard from Dad. He said that the Spencer building is the same way. Not a speck of dust anywhere. And the roof, which was going to have to be replaced, is done as well." She rolled over on top of him and he held her there. "What did that? I mean, other than the two of us, why did the magic clean that up?"

"Just before Kilian told me to release it, I was thinking about how the place was going to help everyone. But it would be delayed by months because of the work that needed to be done on both places." He nodded. "So, when the magic rolled around and over me, I could see it. The buildings were complete. There were people working in them and making the product. Trucks were backed up to the doors, and we were loading and unloading. I could see it, all of it working." Jason told her he'd seen it too, but not understood it. "This is some serious magic."

"It is." Jason brushed the hair off her forehead and kissed her there as he continued. "You know what we're doing today?"

"Yes. We're going to get married. Finally. And no one is going to mess it up this time. Right?" He kissed her again, his body complaining that it was too much. "You really want to do this? Marry this child of a piece of dung?"

"I do believe that I do." He smiled at her. "My dad said that he'd be there as well. And Kilian has agreed to act as the other witness. My brothers, of course, will be there because they told me that you were becoming their sister, and they needed to be sure that I didn't fuck things up for them. Then you and I are going on a nice honeymoon to Europe."

"I've never been. I'm so excited. I got my passport yesterday." He smiled and told her that was good. "I know. You do know that since we have our own plane, I'm bringing back a lot of gifts. Christmas is only five months away."

They were both still laughing when they got in the shower

together. Jason scrubbed her back and washed her hair, but they didn't make love again. He wanted tonight to be special, their wedding night, and if she took him like she had earlier, he'd not be able to stand, much less perform.

Dressing, he thought of all the plans he'd made for the day. After the wedding, they were going to have a lovely lunch with his family, her family now too. Then the plane was ready to take them all around the world. Jason was excited to show her things that he'd seen when they were built. Going down to the kitchen while she finished dressing, he asked if things were about finished here.

"Yes. I've had the cake delivered to the restaurant. And the staff is going to be waiting for you two to enter before they shower you with their blessings. It was most kind of you, sir, to allow us to be a part of it." Jason told him that he was as much family to them as his brothers and dad were. "Thank you. That means a great deal to us."

On the ride to the courthouse she fussed with her flowers, hair, and dress. When he finally took her hands into his, she smiled at him.

"I'm a little nervous." He laughed. "Okay, a lot nervous. I'm worried that when he asks if anyone wants to say something about us not marrying, someone will and I'll have to kill them."

"Not before I do. And no one there will object." She nodded and he watched her face, knowing that she didn't believe him. "Jewel, you're going to be my wife, today. It would have been sooner if life hadn't taken us for a ride, but today is a wonderful day."

"What's the date?" He had to think and told her. "Oh my, my parents, they were married on this date as well. I didn't

even think of that until just this minute. Jason, we're going to
be just fine. It's like we've picked the perfect day of all days
to do this."

"I think so as well." They held hands all the way to the
ceremony, and when the car stopped, he pulled her to him for
a kiss. "I love you, Jewel. And I'm so glad that you are going
to be with me for the rest of our days."

"I am too. I love you very much."

When he thought back to all the terrible things he'd done
and said to her, he cringed. He'd been a bastard, just as she
had called him, several times. "I'm so sorry for all the mean
and horrific things I said and did to you. I wasn't a nice person.
I want to make it up to you, for the rest of my life."

"Okay." He laughed, he just couldn't help it. She was a
delight, and he loved her for it. "Did you think that I'd just let
you get away with that crap?"

"No, but since it's our wedding day, I thought you'd be
a little more forgiving." She told him not a chance. "I can see
that you're going to be a handful, aren't you?"

"You know it. And when we get back from out trip, I
want to see about having a child with you. As soon as we
possibly can." She left him there, in the limo by himself. The
driver cleared his throat and he finally got out.

"I love her." The man grinned and said that was obvious.
"She's never going to let me think I have the upper hand. Nor
do I think she's going to be easy. She's perfect for me. I feel
like an important man today."

"That's the best kind, sir. The perfect ones. And my
momma, God rest her soul, she used to say that it's nice to be
important, but it's more important to be nice." Jason told him
he liked that. "Thank you, sir. My momma wasn't perfect, but

she sure could make you feel good about most anything you did."

The wedding was simple, but exactly what they wanted. His brothers had shown up, and all of them were dressed in their finest with a single rose on their lapels. His dad too. Kilian looked like the queen that she was, and Jason was happy that she remembered to bring a bouquet for Jewel.

As soon as the short service was over, the bouquet, really a bunch of small faeries, left her hands to fly above their head. They dropped seeds over the small gathering, which burst into flowers as soon as they touched the two of them. He'd never been so happy in all his days.

"I have a gift for you both. I thought of giving you crowns to wear, but I thought that too much." Kilian took their hands into hers. "I give you this as protection. Not just from humans, but anyone meaning to cause you harm."

The rings were a thin band made of the most brilliant metal. They weren't silver, at least he didn't think so, but they were beautiful. The designs that circled them were in great detail that showed faeries, with wings dancing around them.

"They're beautiful." Jewel kissed the queen on the cheek as she continued. "I thank you for this. And for all that you've done for us. You are forever welcome in our lives and our home."

"Thank you." Kilian looked slightly embarrassed. "I've never...well, it's been a very long time since I've been welcomed so well. I promise you that good things are coming to the two of you. Be safe on your travels."

They were on the plane when he realized that they were going on their honeymoon. He was married. And had a wife that was as powerful, if not more so, than he was. Laughing, he wondered what was in store for the rest of them. Because he had no doubt that his brothers were about to find their mates as well.

CHAPTER 13

Grayson wasn't sure where he'd gone wrong today. Perhaps it had started when he woke in the wrong bed. He wasn't one to spend the night at a woman's house, but he'd been having fun with her and had ended up back at her place. Something that was never going to happen again.

She'd been clingy and wanted him to stay with her all day. Breakfast, she told him, was what she wanted, then they could go shopping. Grayson didn't shop. If he couldn't buy it online, then he didn't get it. Then there was a mention of going on a long trip, just the two of them. Grayson erased himself from her memories and left as soon as he could. Christ, he just wanted to have some fun.

As he walked through the plant, he thought of all the things that he needed to do today. First, was to make sure that all the correct paperwork was filled out on the employees. He was headed to the dying materials department now to see about one of them that hadn't filled out anything.

Bethany Smith. He had no idea why, but he thought the name was fake. Beth Smith couldn't be any less conspicuous than if she'd have been Jane Doe. When he entered the room where the fruits and vegetables were being cooked to make the dyes, he stopped to watch. It was the best smelling work area he'd ever been in. And over the centuries, Grayson had been in a lot of work areas.

The woman that he was looking for was standing over a pot of carrots. Or that's what he thought they were. Sweet potatoes, it turned out, made a pretty shade of orange that was needed to make some of the holiday bags that were set to ship out. He touched his finger to her shoulder and she turned to look at him.

"I was wondering if you could come with me to fill out some paperwork." Her face took on a look of pure terror. "It's just a few places on your application you neglected to fill out. If you could come with me now, I'm sure we can work it out quickly and you can get back to work."

The language was rapid and loud. Several of the other employees had stopped to look at them, and he felt his face heat up. He didn't have any idea what she was saying, but he had a feeling that it wasn't particularly kind. As she continued to talk to him, he looked around for help. There didn't seem to be anyone coming to aid him.

"It's just a few places that need to be filled out." She grabbed his tie and he had no choice but to follow. All sorts of things were running through his head as he trailed behind her, his clipboard in his hand. "Are you planning to kill me? I can tell you right now that I won't be an easy mark."

She said something else to him. He didn't know why, but he thought she was understanding him very well and making fun of him. As they entered the dining room—breakroom, he supposed it was called—Beth took him to the room's only occupant...a woman sitting with a book in front of her and wearing a set of old headphones. He doubted that she was listening to anything or reading. It was more than likely a way to keep people away.

The woman looked up from her book and pulled the headphones off. He could hear Latin coming from the set, and wondered what she was doing. When she turned them off and leaned back in her chair, the first thing that Grayson thought of was beautiful. Then a profound sorrow. Beth started talking again, but to the woman this time.

"She wants to know if you're going to fire her." He shook his head and sat when Beth did. "I didn't invite you to join me. I'm only answering her question."

"Beth didn't fill out her paperwork correctly. I'm trying to get her to finish it up so she can get paid." The other woman spoke to Beth. "Do you have a name?"

"I'm reasonably sure that everyone does. Otherwise, it would be difficult to get anyone's attention, don't you think?" Before he could answer that, if there was an answer, she continued. "Beth said to tell you that if you're going to be working on the floors and coming up to strangers, that you shouldn't be dressed like a Fed. She's right, you know. Shirt and tie here is a no-no."

"I don't own any jeans." The woman nodded. "Ask her if she can come to the office with me or if we can do it right here. I don't care. I just have a list of names that I have to follow up on."

After speaking to Beth again, the woman turned to him. He had a feeling that he was being sized up, and for some reason she'd found him lacking. Reaching to his collar, he pulled off his tie and set it on the table. The two women spoke quickly and quietly, giving him a chance to look around.

The breakroom had been here when Jewel opened the doors. It had been easy to get someone to come in and cook a few meals, set out some drinks, and take money. It was doing well, he thought, having hot food for some of the workers who he thought might not otherwise get one.

"Beth wants to know what you want her to fill out. She would like for me to read it over to see if it's something that she can do on her own." He nodded and handed it to the woman. "Emerald."

"I'm sorry, what?" She told him her name was Emerald. "That's beautiful. I'm betting that you were named that for the color of your eyes."

"Doubtful. But if you say so. Beth needs her purse for her paperwork. She said that she'd meet you at the office. And if you want to make a good impression, drop the jacket too. You're scaring everyone." She put the headphones back on and looked at the book in front of her. He said her name and she glanced up at him. "I'm on my break. She understands now."

"Are you reading and listening to a book?" She told him she was. "You're not terribly friendly, are you? I'm just trying to figure out something about the people that work for us."

"Emerald Hunter, twenty-eight, single, five foot eleven. I work from five in the morning until four, take a one hour break, do my job, and I don't bother anyone, like some people I know." He laughed. He had no idea why he thought it was funny, but she apparently didn't. "What is it you want from me?"

"What language was Beth speaking?" She told him Portuguese. "What other languages do you speak?"

"You taking a survey or just nosey?" He told her both. "Whatever you need. I have an ear for them."

He spoke to her in Latin, the language of the book she was

190

listening to. She answered him the same way. Then he tried French, Italian, as well as Mandarin. Each time she answered the same way with the same comment. "Leave me alone."

By the time he made it back to his office to help Beth fill out her paperwork, he was in a much better frame of mind. Talking to Emerald was like battling a great warrior, but he had enjoyed it. For every question he had there was a sharp answer, along with her telling him to go away. In the end, she'd left him there in favor of going back to work.

It was close to four when he decided to head to the front time clock. He didn't know why he wanted to bait her more, but he found that he just enjoyed it too much not to give it one more shot. He'd also looked up her employee file.

Nowhere on it did it mention that she spoke several languages. In the space where it asked, he knew it was optional, but she'd left it blank. He wondered on that. Also, her address was only a post office box and not an address. Grayson was going to ask her about that as well.

He saw her walking toward him at five after four. Emerald exuded defensiveness. She walked alone, her head down and her ever present headphones on her ears. He wondered again if she was listening to a book while reading one when she saw him.

"I was wondering if you'd like to get a cup of coffee." She clocked out and stared at him. "It's just a cup of coffee. No harm in it."

"What do you want from me?" He asked her what she meant. "You can't be that dense. I don't want to be bothered. I do my job, work hard, and I stay out of trouble. Not that there is any here, but I really do want to be left alone."

"I like you." She snorted. "Please, I don't know what it

is about you, but I want to spend time with you. Talk to you about why you're listening to Latin on your headphones and reading a book too. I want to know why you are standoffish, how come you speak several languages fluently, and why you're not working someplace that can use your talents. But I would really like to get to know you."

"I promise you, you do not. I'm learning Latin by reading what they're saying on the tape to compare with the words in the book. It's a gift, I guess. I don't like people. Not a good answer, but the only one that I have. They usually aren't as tenacious as you are, but they leave me alone. I speak several languages because I bore easily, and this gives me something to do. I have an eidetic memory. Do you know what that is?" He nodded. "Well good. One less thing I have to explain to you."

"Why are you working here? I'm sure there are places that you can go and use what you have that would certainly pay better." She looked longingly at the door, and Grayson had a feeling that she was hiding out. Not just from a person, but perhaps a group of people. "I can help you. Whatever is going on, I can help you. I have resources that can keep you out of trouble with someone. If that's what is going on with you."

"No one can." She left him standing there then. Just turning on her heel, pulling the headphones back up over her ears, and walking out the door.

Grayson thought about following her, just to see where she lived, when he realized that she'd avoided touching him. Even when he'd tried to take her hand earlier to thank her, she'd not touched him. He had a feeling that not only did she know what he was, but a great deal more about him than he did her.

~~~

Emerald made her way home. It really wasn't that far, but she kept her eyes open for anyone following her. The man at the plant, Grayson Crosby, was going to tell someone she was here and she'd be so fucked. Or perhaps, she thought, it would be done. She was as tired of running as she was of living.

For the last month she'd stayed on her own, only speaking to as few people as she could, and as she'd told him, staying out of trouble. Beth had been having issues when she first started, not being able to read the labels well, and she'd helped her. Showing her how to compare the numbers on the sheet to those on the vats was all she needed. The woman was there to stay with her daughter and children, as her home had been destroyed in the last rain season. That had worked out well for her.

The vampire was going to cause her some trouble, she knew it. He'd been nice enough, even though she'd done her best to be as nasty as she could to him. And Beth did need help with her paperwork. She spoke some English, not well or a lot, but she understood it better. The man had terrified her, Beth told her, because of the way he'd come up behind her.

Emerald was nearly home when she saw the man from yesterday. He'd been hanging out around her building for a couple of days, walking back and forth with a grocery cart. But he wasn't really homeless, nor did he sleep in the alleys behind the buildings where a lot of people lived. He was one of the people, and it didn't matter which group was looking for her.

Emerald wondered if his kind, whatever he was, thought

that she was stupid. She wasn't. Far from it. Even the lady, Carla, who was pushing a cart in the opposite direction from the man, knew he wasn't homeless. It was his shoes.

New tennis shoes with perfect laces wasn't the only tell. He also wore a dirty coat that cost as much if not more than the tie that Grayson had worn. Making something messy did not hide the quality of the material.

His cart wasn't new, not that that was a good sign. Most of the people who employed carts as their means of keeping track of their things got older ones, those that the stores had pushed to the side because they were broken or nearly so. And his was filled with car parts. A headlight and an old tire that was bald. As well as two empty soda cans that were too expensive for anyone out here to afford. He was a moron.

He spoke into his sleeve when he saw her and Emerald moved into the first building. It wasn't hers, but it would do for now. As he abandoned his cart in favor of going after her, Emerald knocked on the door of the first apartment. When no one answered her knocks, she went to the next and then the next until she was let in. All she needed was access to one of the rooms, then she could get away.

The window that she was going out of led onto a fire escape. Climbing out onto it, she handed the woman in the room some cash. It wasn't much, but it would buy her time. It took her seconds to climb the first flight of stairs, and she heard the man pounding on the door to the apartment she had just left. Emerald made it to the rooftop and looked to the ground.

There were three cars parked in the alley, all of them black sedans with dark windows. She knew who they were and what they wanted with her, but she was in no way going with them. Not again. Leaping to the next building, she landed hard on her knee and winced at the pain. She was getting too old for this shit. There were more cars between this building and her own.

"Fuck." What do to? What to do?

The vampire. She didn't want to trust him, really had no reason to, but she did. Reaching out to him, hoping she wasn't making a mistake, she touched his mind just as he was getting into his car for the day.

It's Emerald. He stiffened and she had to smile. *You might not be able to talk to me unless we exchange touches, but I don't have to wait that long. I'm in trouble. Deep shit here.*

Can I help you? She wasn't sure and told him what she was up against. *All right. Can you get to Third Street? Or is that going to lead you right to these men?*

He hadn't asked, not once, about why she had men chasing her. She wasn't sure if that was a good thing or not, but had to do something. She wasn't worried about dying, but she didn't want to suffer like she knew these men would make her do if they caught her.

I can get there. But if you don't see me, then move on. I'll find you. He told her what kind of truck he was driving and the plate number. *I'm really trusting you here. If you fuck with me, I have all kinds of special ways of killing you.*

I'm an immortal. She told him she was as well. *All right. But I want some answers when we get to safety. Please?*

Yeah, sure. And if I can get out of this in one piece, then I might trust you more with the answers you're not going to like. He said he was all right with that as well. *We'll see.*

She leapt to the next building and her knee hurt her. Emerald sat there for several seconds and knew that she had to get going. The shot that rang out got her up and moving. They were getting serious now.

Going into her apartment from the window was easy enough. Killing the man that stood outside it hadn't been. Throwing his body to the ground below, she went inside, grabbed her duffle, and pressed the button.

In ten seconds the warning alerts would go off in each apartment. Then hopefully everyone would get out before it blew. The men outside, the ones that were looking for her, wouldn't hear a thing until it was too late. She was at the third building when she heard the explosion.

Grayson was at the corner of Third and Main. She watched him for a few minutes to make sure that he'd not been followed. The bullet that she'd taken as she was leaving her building was hurting her badly, but she knew that she'd heal soon enough.

As soon as she approached his truck, she saw the man coming out of the bakery. Lifting her hands up, she was ready to kill him when Grayson saw her. She wanted to warn him, to tell him to get out of the way, when she realized that they looked alike. The man, older by a couple of years she'd bet, called out his name. The same trust she had for Grayson didn't extend to him, but she had a feeling that they were related. Getting in the bed of the truck, she lay there while the other man got in the cab. They were moving when Grayson spoke to her.

This is my brother, Chase. She didn't speak, her body was shutting down to heal. *He doesn't have any idea what is going on. May I share with him?*

I'm going to trust you. I haven't any idea why, but I'm going to. I must get somewhere dark and cold. I need cold. He said that he had a basement. *That'll work. I won't be able to...I'm hurt and I need to heal. If someone comes looking for me, don't give me to them. I don't care to live, but I don't want to die by their hands, if possible.*

So, you're not a true immortal. She said that removing his head would kill him too. *Very good point. All right. I'm taking you to my basement. It's cold down there, and I can make it colder if you need it.*

Yes. The colder the better. She was fighting to stay awake. If they were attacked, she could help them to safety. *You can't tell anyone where I am. It will mean death to so many.*

~~~

Chase lifted the woman up and held her. He knew what she was to him, had since he'd wrapped her up in the cab's blanket to hide her when Grayson had pulled over. She was his mate, and she wasn't human. He looked at Grayson when he said his name.

"You have to take us to my house. I have that walk-in freezer." He asked him if he thought that might be too cold. "No, I don't."

"Do you know what she is?" He nodded. "Well, do you want to share that information, or are you going to stand there and hold her until I lock you both in the back of the truck and leave?"

"Ice dragon. She's an ice dragon." Grayson took a step back, knowing as well as he did how powerful they were. "And she's my mate."

"Christ." He nodded. Chase wasn't sure what to do now but to take her home and put her in his freezer. "Let's get her someplace safe for now, then we'll talk."

"She's being chased, you said." Grayson nodded. "They must know what she is. Or have an idea. They'll tear her apart to use her."

They got in the truck. Chase held her in his arms while his brother drove. His mate was a dragon. He had no idea what to do nor what to say to her. She was as old, if not older, than him. Taking her wrist to his mouth, he took a small bite of her, just enough that he could feel her when she needed him. Not that he had any idea what he could do for someone like her, but he sealed up the wounds and lay his head back on the seat.

"She told me she was twenty-eight. I'm assuming that that's not quite true." Chase said more than likely not. "She also said that she had an eidetic memory, that's why she knows so many languages. I can believe that, but I think it's more than that. She spoke them flawlessly."

"I don't know a lot about her kind other than what you read in horror books. They're said to lure unsuspecting people into their lair and kill them. I read one book once that said that she can freeze a person with a glance. I don't know that it's not true, so I'm going to try my best not to piss her off." Grayson said that sounded like a good plan. "She works for Jewel, I take it."

"Yes, she did. I don't think she'll be able to go back there. And if she does, the rest of us might not be safe. Whoever was after her, they weren't playing around. They wanted her badly." Chase asked him about the explosion. "Her, I would imagine. I don't know...as I said, I don't know a great deal about her."

When he got to his home, he put her right in the freezer. He didn't know what else to do, so he brought in several of the pillows from his couch and put them under her head. When he'd done all that he could do for her, he closed the door and sat down. Grayson sat across from him.

"I wish that Jason was here." Chase nodded. "Not that he'd know any more than we do, but he might have some insight on her kind. Dad might know some."

"For right now, I'd rather just keep this between the two of us. For a few minutes, anyway. If Dad were to know that I've found my mate, he'd be all over this. And I need to think." Grayson leaned back in the chair but said nothing. "She's a dragon, Grayson. An ice dragon."

"You said that." Chase looked at the freezer, then got up to pace. "Does it bother you that you're mated to her, or mated period?"

"I don't know why what she is should matter. I'm a little afraid, if you want to know the truth. But no, I don't mind having a mate." Grayson nodded. "Those people after her, did she tell you what they might want from her?"

"No. And you should also know that she spoke to me without any contact. Not even a touch. Also, she did say that she didn't mind dying, but not by their hands. She seemed to imply that they'd remove her head when they found her." Chase nodded and kept walking. "How long do you suppose she needs to be in there?"

Before he could answer, the freezer opened and there she stood. Chase took a step back, but couldn't stop staring at her. She was naked, her body covered in a thick ice that looked like clothing. Even her head was encased in a helmet-like crystal that looked to be armor too. But it was her eyes that captured him. They were as green as the stone she was named for. And just as hard looking.

Chase dropped to his knees in front of her. The need to submit was strong, and he looked up at her. She had a sword in her hand, a dragon shape for a hilt, the blade dark with what appeared to be blood. When she looked at him, he smiled.

"You're my mate." He nodded, still unable to get his mouth moving around the dryness of it. "You're going to be in big trouble, I'm afraid."

"Yeah, I think so too." The sword disappeared and the ice was replaced with her clothing again. "Welcome to our home, Emerald. I'm glad to have found you."

"You would think that. You're as addled as your brother. There are people after me that wish to take me apart. They'll want you too now." He had already figured that out. "I need to rest for a few more days. Will that be a problem?"

He told her to take all the time she needed. When she nodded and moved back into the freezer, he looked at Grayson. He looked as poleaxed as he felt.

"I guess we should tell the rest of them now." Grayson nodded, still staring at the closed door. "Grayson, we have to protect her while she rests."

"Yes, I can help. But who's going to protect us from her?"

Chase laughed. It was all he could do. He was so fucked right now that he wasn't sure which way was up. But he did have a mate, and that made it somewhat better.

Paranormal Romance with a Bite!

BLOOD, BODY AND MIND:
A KATHI S. BARTON PARANORMAL ROMANCE

YOUR FREE COPY IS WAITING...

Aaron MacManus, the new master vampire of the realm just wanted to go out and meet some of his subjects and to figure out what needed to be done to set things right.

April and Demetrius Carlovetti own an air service and are the most trusted and well liked vampires in Aaron's realm. What he didn't expect when he visited them was betrayal. His own bodyguards try to murder him and blame it on the Carlovetti's.

Sara Temple was not a vampire. She pilots planes for the Carlovetti Airways. She had secretes of her own and working for this small air service is keeping her out of sight. The last thing she wanted to do was save a vampire, even an extremely good looking one.

Sara was only trying to survive but with Aaron she becomes embroiled in politics, the magic of several realms involving a queen in peril, magical beings, passion and love.

Blood, Body and Mind, the first book in the Aaron's Kiss series.

Get Your Free Book!

http://eepurl.com/brCBvP

Before You Go...

HELP AN AUTHOR

write a review

THANK YOU!

Share your voice and help guide other readers to these wonderful books. Even if it's only a line or two your reviews help readers discover the author's books so they can continue creating stories that you'll love. Login to your favorite retailer and leave a review. Thank you.

AWARD WINNING, BESTSELLING AUTHOR

Kathi Barton, winner of the Pinnacle Book Achievement award as well as a best-selling author on Amazon and All Romance books, lives in Nashport, Ohio with her husband Paul. When not creating new worlds and romance, Kathi and her husband enjoy camping and going to auctions. She can also be seen at county fairs with her husband who is an artist and potter.

Her muse, a cross between Jimmy Stewart and Hugh Jackman, brings her stories to life for her readers in a way that has them coming back time and again for more. Her favorite genre is paranormal romance with a great deal of spice. You can visit Kathi online and drop her an email if you'd like. She loves hearing from her fans. aaronskiss@gmail.com.

Follow Kathi on her blog: http://kathisbartonauthor. blogspot.com/

Printed in the USA
CPSIA information can be obtained
at www.ICGtesting.com
LVHW051614020124
767983LV00008B/407